"It always helps to laugh a little, Angie."

Sonny tried reasoning with her. He didn't want to talk about the kiss they'd just shared.

"I don't feel like laughing. My life is all jumbled up!" Angie began pacing again. "I don't know how I feel about anything anymore...."

Sonny started to get up from the couch to take her into his arms, but he held himself back. "I think that's part of the healing," he said softly.

"I don't want to be healing. It just doesn't seem fair."

He ached for her. "Healing is part of life, honey. We have to."

"I'll tell you what we have to do...." Angie sighed raggedly. "We have to stop spending so much time together. That's going to get us both into trouble...."

Dear Reader,

A gift from the heart, from us to you—this month's special collection of love stories, filled with the spirit of the holiday season. And what better place to find romance this time of year than UNDER THE MISTLETOE?

In *Daddy's Angel,* favorite author Annette Broadrick spins a tale full of charm and magic—and featuring FABULOUS FATHER Bret Bishop. Treetop angel Noelle St. Nichols visits this single dad and the children she's cherished from afar—and suddenly longs to trade her wings for love.

Annie and the Wise Men by Lindsay Longford is the heartwarming story of Annie Conroy and her kids, as their search for a temporary home on the holiday lands them face-to-face with a handsome young "Scrooge," Ben Jackson.

And Carla Cassidy will persuade you to believe once again that Santa Claus is not only alive and well—he's in love! Someone up above must have known that rugged Chris Kringle was just the man to make Julie Casswell smile again. Could it have been *The Littlest Matchmaker?*

More great books to look for this month include *A Precious Gift* by Jayne Addison, continuing the story of the lovable Falco family. Moyra Tarling shows us that *Christmas Wishes* really do come true in a moving story of a father reunited with his son by a spirited woman who believes in love. And there's love, laughter and merrymaking unlimited in Lauryn Chandler's *Romantics Anonymous.*

Wishing you a happy holiday and a wonderful New Year!

Anne Canadeo
Senior Editor

A PRECIOUS GIFT

Jayne Addison

ROMANCE™

Published by Silhouette Books

America's Publisher of Contemporary Romance

For my father and Terry

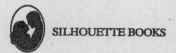 SILHOUETTE BOOKS

ISBN 0-373-08980-5

A PRECIOUS GIFT

Copyright © 1993 by Jane Atkin

Books by Jayne Addison

Silhouette Romance

You Made Me Love You #888
†*Something Blue* #944
†*A Precious Gift* #980

† The Falco Family

JAYNE ADDISON

lives on the North Shore of Long Island with her husband, Jerome. Their three children, Steven, Andrew and Beth, are presently attending colleges away from home. Between running up huge phone bills talking to the kids, and a full-time job as a salesperson/ bookkeeper for a local builder, Jayne fills her free time writing romance fiction. It's one way to beat the empty-nest syndrome.

THE FALCO FAMILY

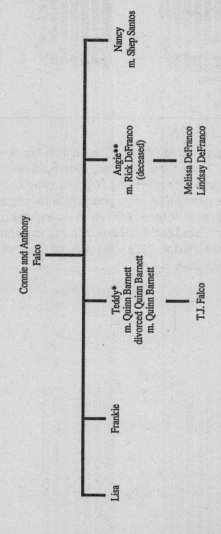

Connie and Anthony Falco

Lisa

Frankie

Teddy*
m. Quinn Barnett
divorced Quinn Barnett
m. Quinn Barnett

T.J. Falco

Angie**
m. Rick DeFranco
(deceased)

Melissa DeFranco
Lindsay DeFranco

Nancy
m. Shep Santos

* Something Blue
** A Precious Gift

Chapter One

At the sound of her doorbell, Angie DeFranco pushed her bangs out of her eyes and walked from her living room to answer it. A little more messy for the abuse, her reddish-brown hair fell right back down on her temple.

She opened the door.

"Hi." Sonny DeFranco scowled slightly.

"What?" Angie shot an irritated look at her brother-in-law. "What's wrong?"

"You didn't ask who was there before you opened the door."

"I peeked first." Angie jerked a thumb toward the peephole.

"I didn't see you peek." He knew she was lying. Her face always took on a flush when she was lying.

Angie shrugged rather than elaborate on her fib. He

was right to admonish her. She even admonished herself. Except for this one time, she always checked before opening her door. "The girls aren't here. They're staying over at my mother's house."

"I guess I should have called." He didn't make any move to leave. "As long as I'm here, why don't I take a look at your dishwasher?"

"I told you yesterday that I was going to call a repairman." She wasn't in the mood to entertain.

"Have you called someone yet?"

"Not exactly."

Sonny kept his post. He'd been around her a lot in the year and a half since his older brother had been killed on duty. They didn't always get along one-to-one. "Let me give it a try. Those repair guys charge a fortune and it might be something really simple, like a loose screw."

Angie studied him. He was actively cocksure of himself in a way that was perfectly acceptable for an undercover detective with the NYPD. The cocksure part of his personality bothered her every so often. "All right." She stepped aside to let him in. It wasn't worth a lengthy discussion.

"Do you have a screwdriver?"

"There's one in a drawer in the kitchen." Following him, Angie found herself doing what she often did, and that was comparing him to Rick. He was shorter. His hair wasn't as dark as Rick's. His eyes were blue. Rick's had been gray. Except for occasional mannerisms, the two hadn't resembled each other at all. But they had been exceptionally close.

Sonny took off his denim jacket and dropped it on one of the cane kitchen chairs. Angie found a screwdriver and was just handing it to him when her doorbell rang again. He leveled a warning gaze at her. She looked back at him with eyes that held a hint of impetuousness. "Who's there?" she called deliberately loud, and then left him to find out.

Her sister Nancy responded behind the door, but it wasn't just Nancy who filed in.

Angie's four siblings greeted Angie with smiles and hugs, then took seats in the living room. None of them seemed to notice their sister's agitation. Standing in the center of the room, Angie regarded them with her fiercest stare. "Okay, whose idea was this? Did Mom set this up?"

Nancy Santos, the oldest at thirty-three, answered. "Yes. She called each of us and said drop whatever you're doing, go over there and gang up on her." Nancy smiled, but then gave Angie her most pragmatic look. "She'll leave you alone if we can talk reason into you..."

"To get Mom off your case has to be worth something," Teddy Falco inserted, offering a teasing grin. Her brother was three years younger than Nancy, a year and a couple of months younger than Angie.

"Lisa and I can attest to that," Frankie Falco, twenty-seven, gave the baby of the family, twenty-one-year-old Lisa, a poke. Lisa Falco poked him right back.

Angie tossed her head, trying to get her bangs from her eyes. She couldn't remember the last time she'd sat in a beauty parlor. She'd taken to chopping her hair herself. "I'll tell Mom that you talked reason into me. All you have to do is back me up. Please tell her to stop giving my name and phone number out."

Lisa laughed. "I thought she only did that to me."

"Did you hear from the guy whose mother has a condition?" Angie asked piquantly.

Lisa slowly shook her head. "What kind of condition?"

"I don't know." Angie rolled her vivid brown eyes. "Mom just told me that he was going to call, but not to get too close, too soon. 'His mother has a condition.' Then she said that she and Daddy were checking to see if it could be inherited." Angie used her hands to emphasize her aggravation.

In the kitchen, Sonny grinned. He could hear the conversation in the living room—not that he was eavesdropping.

"You didn't go out with him, did you?" Frankie questioned. He was a smaller, quirkier version of Teddy. Both men drew women like bees to honey, but Teddy was taken and not noticing anymore. Frankie was the one with the active hive.

Angie lifted a shoulder in outrage. "No, I didn't go out with him. I'm not interested in dating."

Nancy sighed. "You're too young to stop living."

"I haven't stopped living," Angie retorted. "I loved Rick, and I'm not going to love anyone else."

A hazy image of Rick at sixteen came into Sonny's mind. His brother, Sonny remembered, had been positively mooney-eyed over Angie right from the start.

"How can you say that?" Lisa asked. "You haven't given yourself a chance to meet anyone."

"I know how hard it is," Nancy interjected. "You and Rick started going together back in high school. You hardly ever dated anyone else."

Angie slouched down on a lavender armchair. "I never thought it would happen . . . He loved being on the force. I worried when he left for work, but I never really thought that one day he wouldn't come home. . . ."

Sonny felt her ache and his own.

"Hey," Teddy murmured gently. Leaving the floral armchair where he'd been sitting, he hunkered down next to her, and put his hand alongside her face. "Let us help you, Angie."

Angie pulled in a breath, and forced her mouth to turn up slightly at the corners. "You've all helped me. I'm fine. Really . . ."

There was a crashing sound from the kitchen. Everyone jumped. Sonny pushed open the swinging door into the dining room, which was a section of the living room. "Don't worry," he assured, picking Angie out with his eyes. "I've got it under control."

"Hey, Sonny. We didn't know you were here," Frankie called over. "What are you up to?"

"I'm fixing Angie's dishwasher."

Angie wondered if there was going to be anything left for a repairman when Sonny got through. She did remind herself that it was generous of him to try.

"Need any help?" Teddy asked.

"No, I'm fine." Sonny stepped back into the kitchen, letting the door close.

Teddy went back to his seat. "Rick wouldn't want you spending the rest of your life alone, and he'd want a man around for the girls."

Angie met Teddy's concerned gaze. "You're around, and Frankie is around. Sonny comes around whenever he can. He's been terrific with Melissa and Lindsay." She raised her voice, pitching the last of her response toward the kitchen. She hoped Sonny could hear her. She not only meant it, but she owed him a compliment to make up for having been so grouchy with him before.

Taken by surprise at her nicety toward him, Sonny nearly shaved his finger with the screwdriver. But he smiled.

"We're not talking about the girls right now. We're talking about you." Nancy took over again. "You haven't gone shopping with me in ages. You've lost so much weight. Your clothes are just hanging on you. You're going to start looking like one of those old women who walks around in black stockings with a kerchief around her head."

Angie thought of her Aunt Tessa, who looked just like that. Only, Aunt Tessa was old—almost eighty. Was that what she had to look forward to?

"I'm going to start eating better. I promise." Angie glanced down at herself. The jeans she was wearing used to hug her figure. Now, they were belted and baggy. She'd let her pink pinstripe shirt hang out to disguise the fact that her jeans didn't have belt loops.

For a few seconds they all listened to hiss of the radiator pipes. The landlord of the Riverdale garden apartment complex was not stingy with heat. It wasn't even all that cold out yet.

Angie inhaled deeply and surveyed the faces around her. She adored them, but she didn't want to deal with the subject they were on. "Lisa, it's got to be close to five, and it's Saturday. Don't you have a date to get ready for?" She was hoping to get them to leave, if not in unison, at least one at a time.

Lisa nodded. "I do have to leave in a few minutes. He's picking me up at seven-thirty. I don't want to be late for my first date with the guy."

Frankie razzed. "Is this another guy that Mom and Dad will detest?"

Nancy spoke before Lisa had the chance. "We can figure that's a given."

Lisa flicked her dark, permed, shoulder-length hair. "Do you want me to spoil my record?"

"Let's not get off the subject." Teddy called the group to order. "We can work on Lisa after we finish with Angie."

Sonny didn't need to see Angie's face to know that by this point she was gritting her teeth.

Lisa got to her feet and put her black blazer on over her white turtleneck sweater and black stirrup pants. "I'm going now, before you all get the chance to start on me."

There were hugs all around. They were a demonstrative family.

Teddy groaned. "I'm praying that I never have a daughter."

Nancy sent Teddy a grin. "You'll be just like Daddy if you do. You and Frankie could come and go whenever you wanted. Angie and I were always under lock and key. We were docile about it. Lisa has always given Daddy a run for the money."

Angie gave a smile that was triggered by her sister's reminiscence. "Nancy, I wasn't always docile. Do you remember the time I climbed out our bedroom window?"

"And down the cherry tree," Nancy added, filling out the picture.

Sonny smiled broadly, picturing Angie shimmying down a tree. He remembered her tomboy phase. They'd practically grown up together. She'd been around his house almost as much as her own.

"You dummy, you went and confessed to Mommy and Daddy afterward," Nancy said as she recalled the entire incident.

Teddy angled his head toward Angie. "Just look at her... Look how good-looking she is when she's laughing."

She was good-looking, Sonny thought to himself, pausing with the water relay hose in his hand.

"Stop it!" Angie countered. "If you don't stop all of this, I am never going to laugh again."

Nancy exhaled a sigh. "I have to get home. Shep and I promised the twins we'd take them out for dinner. But you have to promise me, Angie, that you'll go shopping with me one day next week. We'll have lunch out... maybe dinner. We can take in a movie, or get tickets for a show."

Sonny felt remiss that he hadn't once suggested taking her out.

"Sounds terrific," Angie agreed, though she was already contemplating coming up with an excuse. It wasn't that she didn't want to spend time with Nancy. She just didn't want to get back on the topic that they were on now. It felt good to her to think she was only meant to love once.

Nancy rose to her feet. "I found this fabulous store. It just opened. Everything is discounted. You're not going to believe the prices."

"I'll go with you if you promise not to pester me about dating." She really did need to do something about her wardrobe.

"Okay." Nancy gave her sister a squeeze and went to the door wrapped in a brand-new green suede cape.

After Nancy left, Angie asked hopefully, "Don't the two of you have to get going?"

"Not yet," Teddy responded.

"I'm not going out tonight until nine," Frankie said.

Angie sat back in her seat, closed her eyes and massaged her eyelids. She worked on mentally willing her brothers to leave.

"Don't you know anyone you can introduce Angie to?" Teddy asked Frankie.

"I don't know anyone that I'd want around her. What about you?"

"Most of the single guys I know are in the business. I'm promoting a guy right now who seems to have it together, but he's not for Angie."

Frankie nodded sagely. "We certainly don't want her getting hooked on a rapper or rocker."

Angie waited a beat. "Why don't the two of you go scouting? Start right now. Line them up for me and I'll look them over." Her fatuousness was ignored.

Sonny swiped the sweat from his forehead with the back of his hand. This job was more difficult than he'd anticipated. He thought about her dating. Frankie and Teddy were right.

"I think she should join some clubs," Teddy suggested.

"What kind of clubs?" Frankie questioned.

"I've looked into it," Teddy replied. "There's one for single parents."

Frankie clicked his tongue to the roof of his mouth. "Do you think she's experienced enough not to pick out some jerk?"

Angie jumped up. "That's it! I've had it..." Marching, Angie walked out of the living room, down the hall to her bedroom. She slammed and locked the door.

Teddy followed Frankie to the closed door. "Hey, moppet," Frankie called out. "How about I cancel my date, and take you out for dinner? What do you say?"

"No," Angie screamed from her bed. She was sprawled out facedown. Her voice was muffled, but it carried.

"Come home with me," Teddy said. "Quinn is cooking. You can help me suffer through it."

"No," Angie yelled. "Just go. Leave me alone! I want to be alone."

Frankie and Teddy looked at each other. Frankie shrugged. Teddy seconded the motion.

Angie tiptoed to the door. She listened with her ear pressed to the wood. After a few minutes, she was pretty certain she heard the retreating tread of two pairs of sneakered feet.

Angie flopped back down on her bed. She closed her eyes. She was too agitated to think of sleep, but equally too drained of energy to do anything else but lay limp.

The grumbling of her stomach finally got Angie off the bed. The room was hot and stuffy. Going into the adjoining bathroom, Angie splashed cold water on her face. Her hair was damp, tangled and curly. She looked like she was sporting a serving of Chinese lo mein on her head. With food on her mind, Angie estimated that she had to have been in her bedroom for nearly an hour.

Frankie and Teddy were no longer in her living room. She was certain that Sonny was gone by now. Relieved, but lonely, Angie continued through the dining room, and pushed in the swinging door to her kitchen.

Sonny turned. He'd been watching a pot of water, waiting for it to come to a boil. "I figured I'd hang around. I don't have any plans for tonight, and I think you could use some company."

"I don't need any company."

They shared a prolonged stare.

"I think you do." Sonny continued his in-the-eye-look. "You can be prickly with me all you want, but I'm not leaving. Being alone isn't good for you. It doesn't matter that you don't like me all that much."

Angie wrestled to gather her thoughts. "I've never disliked you. We just never got to be that close."

"It's time that we changed that." Sonny stood his ground. "We need each other."

It hadn't struck her until that moment just how much Sonny must still be missing his older brother.

"I hope you're hungry." Sonny glanced at the pot of water that still hadn't come to a boil. "I'm making you one of my specialties."

Angie felt her throat become achingly tight. She almost couldn't swallow. She concentrated on the cleft in Sonny's chin. It was yet another feature that set him apart from Rick. She felt rotten that she hadn't been concerning herself with Sonny's loss. Rick would have wanted her to. "What kind of specialty?"

"Let me surprise you. Sit down."

She was too uptight to sit. "How's the dishwasher?"

"I've got a little bit more to go on it." He looked back at the water in the pot and hoped he could get a plumber in quickly.

"I see." She took note of a pair of mirror-lensed, steel-rimmed sunglasses that he wore year-round. They were popping out of the pocket of his fire-red T-shirt. He had a white sweatband on his right wrist. She guessed he'd played handball at the gym some time before he'd arrived. He and Rick had often played a game or two of handball after work. How she missed that simple sameness in her life! Her eyes brimmed with tears and her body shook. She turned her back to Sonny, trying to get control of herself. It had been a long time since she'd cried. Angrily, Angie wiped at her eyes. She wasn't going to help Sonny by breaking down.

Before Angie had a chance to think of pushing him away, Sonny had come across the room and caught her up in his arms. "It's okay, Angie," he whispered into her ear as she leaned against him. "Cry it out." He plowed his fingers into her thick hair to bring it back off her face.

Even annoyed with herself, she still couldn't stop. Angie cried for a long time, until there were no tears left, and then she sniffled while Sonny softly massaged her back.

"Catch your breath. Try to relax." He drew her closer still.

Absently, she rubbed her cheek against his T-shirt. "I'm getting you all wet."

He kept her arched into his caress. "I haven't washed this one yet. It may not be color fast. But I'm game for a red chest. Being tanned in October is very in. Rotate your face. You're going to want an even look."

Her tension lessened at his joking. Closing her eyes, Angie drew a gulp of air and pressed the opposite side of her face to his chest.

Sonny rocked her. "Teddy and Frankie have a point. You should be dating."

Angie vehemently shook her head against the cords of Sonny's neck. Now that she was breathing regularly, she could smell his clean and soothing scent. The after-shave he used was evident, but not too sweet. She didn't like sweet after-shave.

Sonny locked his fingers together at the small of Angie's back. He could feel how thin she was. "I know what you're thinking. You're thinking that if you went out with some man, you'd be betraying Rick. You have to stop thinking that way. I know Rick wouldn't want you thinking that way."

She was uptight again, and defensive, but she didn't offer to quarrel. She didn't want any more lectures.

"I have some friends I'd like to introduce you to." He'd suggested that possibility to Teddy and Frankie, and they'd agreed on the idea.

"Your friends are too young for me." Her voice quivered.

He smiled against her hair. "All my friends aren't twenty-six. Anyway, a guy of twenty-six doesn't have to be too young for you. What are you now? Thirty-two?" She didn't look anywhere near that.

"Thirty-one and three quarters," Angie sniffled. She was not going to add in those extra few months until she had to, though she felt closer to eighty than thirty-two.

"You look more like twenty. You're almost too young for me. What I mean is..." Suddenly ill at ease, Sonny didn't finish. He thought that he might have sounded as if he was coming on to her, which was the last thing he would have imagined himself doing. She was his sister-in-law...

"I bet most of your friends are cops, and I never want to be involved with another cop... never!"

Sonny had sense enough not to say anything for a time. During the pause, Sonny became consciously aware of her femininity. He shifted himself slightly so that they weren't quite hip-to-hip. When he did speak, he forced a light tone. "How about an accountant, or a lawyer? Someone straight, someone who doesn't walk the edge?" His easygoing blue eyes engaged her puffy bronze gaze.

"Straight would be a requisite if I was looking," Angie retorted, then was shocked that he'd got her to be flip and possibly even flirty. And she was becoming increasingly aware of how intimately he was holding her against himself.

Sonny grinned. "Hey, you're blushing."

"I am not," Angie rebutted. "It's hot in here. Or maybe it's from your shirt."

"You're lying." Sonny flashed his teeth.

Pressing her palms to his chest, Angie levered herself off his shoulders.

He let her go, though he struggled inwardly with his protective instincts. He did think she needed to be held longer. He was sorry that it had taken him so long to give her what his brother would have expected him to give. She needed him as much, if not even more, than the kids did.

She'd heard of the phrase, sex-starved... Was that happening to her? Being held by Sonny hadn't felt at all like being held by one of her brothers.

"I know exactly what you need." Sonny chopped the air between them with his hand to make a point.

"What do I need?" Angie regarded him with a degree of nervousness. Wanting to detach herself from his steady gaze, she glanced down at his straight-legged black jeans and scuffed sneakers.

"A big brother. Someone to look after you. That's where I come in."

"The job is already filled. I have two brothers looking after me."

"I know Teddy and Frankie want to do their part, but Teddy is busy. And Frankie, if you'll forgive me for saying so, is too much a nut job—not that I don't think he's a great guy."

She forgave him without discussion. Frankie *was* a nut job. She'd always thought that Sonny was a nut job as well. "Aren't you busy?"

"I've got nothing going on right now except work. I'd say that you're stuck with me, like it or not." Having assigned himself a task, Sonny was not about to be deterred.

Angie had a retort. "I don't think your girlfriend is going to appreciate being ditched so you can spend time with me."

"We broke up." Sonny shrugged.

"What happened?" Angie was surprised.

"She thought that after eight months, we should start talking about marriage. I thought it was time I took a hike."

Angie narrowed her gaze thoughtfully. "Do you think that you might have a problem with commitment?"

Sonny grinned flippantly. "I wouldn't say I have a problem, but it does seem to be low on my agenda."

Angie had an answer for that. "The right woman will get you to change your mind, but you're not going to meet her hanging out with me."

The phone rang.

Angie made no move to pick it up though there was a receiver right on the wall in the kitchen.

Sonny motioned. "Want me to get it?"

"The machine is on." Angie pointed to the counter.

The answering machine clicked on at that point, and they both listened to the message as it came across.

"Hi, my name is Robert Spitilaire," came a shaky male voice after the beep. "Your mother suggested to my mother that I call you. Oh, and your mother told my mother that I should mention that I'm not the one whose mother has a condition. I'd like to get together. Give me a call. My number is 555-9689."

Sonny lifted his eyebrows. "I say we find out a little more about Robbie before you call him back."

Angie flung her hands in the air. "I say you should mind your own business, Sonny. Anyway, I'm not interested in calling Robbie back."

Sonny's eyes gleamed at her deliberately long. "Weren't you paying attention? I told you that I was making you my business."

Enough was enough. "You can't make me your business unless I want you to make me your business. And I don't want you to make me your business." She threw him an angry glance, but it didn't help.

"I'm not giving you a choice." Sonny crossed his arms in front of his lean abdomen. "Someone has got to get you back into life, and I've volunteered. Ask Teddy and Frankie. They'll tell you we decided that I was the best choice."

"We'll just see about that," Angie warned, giving him a knee-jerk response. Just who did he think he was, barreling over her with his take-charge attitude?

"I guess we will." Sonny tossed her a confident smile. "So, where do you keep your pasta?"

Chapter Two

"Wait a minute," Angie balked. She grabbed Sonny's arm as he went to open the door to Video Magic Dating Service.

Sonny impatiently cocked his head to one side. "Let's not argue again."

Angie made a face. "How did I let you talk me into this?"

"It wasn't easy," Sonny muttered.

Angie tossed a glare his way. "If you're going to take that attitude, I'm going home."

"No way." Sonny glared right back, conveying his frustration. It had taken him three weeks to get her this far. He knew she'd finally capitulated just to shut him up.

Seeing that she wasn't going to sway him with anger, Angie curbed her truculent disposition and changed her tactics. She'd let him turn her into a project because his heart was in the right place. Only she hadn't expected him to wear her down to the point where talk turned into action. "Let's just take a walk around the block. I need a few more minutes to work myself up to this." She gave him her very best smile.

Sonny looked meaningfully into Angie's eyes. He could see them, finally, since she'd gotten her hair cut yesterday. She had great eyes. She didn't need the touch of mascara she'd applied in an afterthought right before they'd left her apartment. "I'll go along with this stall as long as you promise that you are going to go through with it?"

Angie smiled again, knowing she was about to get her way. She was certainly due an inch. "Do you know that you nag worse than my mother?"

"Yeah, yeah." Sonny put his mirrored sunglasses back on. "Do you want a hot chocolate, or a cup of coffee, or something?"

"Yes." Angie's relieved swallow was audible. It made Sonny smile, though he didn't let her notice. She was a handful!

They found a luncheonette just down the street. It was two o'clock and the place was just about empty. He led her to the counter, figuring she'd dawdle more at a booth. The woman behind the counter, who looked to be in her late forties, sent them an inquiring glance blandly chewing a wad of gum.

Sonny extended the inquiry to Angie. "What would you like?"

Angie thought for a second. "An orange soda."

He didn't approve of her choice. "If you want something cold, how about a malted?" He'd been doing his utmost to see to it that she ate better. She was still skin and bones.

"I said, an orange soda." Actually, a malted sounded good to her.

Since he'd decided somewhere midway during the last three weeks to give in on the smaller issues, Sonny didn't push. If nothing else, it was a way to shore up his strength. "An orange soda and a chocolate malted." He gave their order, then fixed his eyes back on Angie while the gumball queen went to work. "Did you eat lunch?"

"I already told you that I did." Angie looked back at Sonny's lenses and volunteered a belligerent jerk of her chin. Her petulant image flashed back at her.

Sonny cracked a relaxed smile. "What did you have?"

"I don't believe this..." Angie groaned. "I wouldn't ask you what you had for lunch."

"I don't consider it too personal a question." He gave her a teasing grin. "I had two slices of pizza. Now, what did you have?"

Angie gritted her teeth. "Tuna on rye," she embellished. She'd had some tuna, but right from the can and only a few forkfuls at best.

She picked up her orange soda right after it was placed on the counter and took a sip.

Sonny raised the silver cylinder and poured himself a glassful of malted. Angie, watching out of the corner of her eye, couldn't keep from noticing that the thick chocolate looked delicious. "Would you like a taste?'' Sonny offered before raising the glass to his lips.

"No, thank you." Her mouth watering, Angie watched Sonny knock it back while she drank more of her orange soda. The artificial citrus was leaving a sour taste in her mouth. She put the glass down without finishing.

"Is that all you're going to drink?" He'd waited a few moments for her to pick her soda back up.

Angie propped her elbow on the counter. "Can I ask you something?"

Sonny grinned. He'd gotten to know her quite well in the last few weeks. She could be a pro at procrastinating when she wanted to be.

"What do you want to know?" At some time today, he was going to get her into that dating service...if he had to drag her in kicking and screaming!

Angie gave his smile her full attention while it continued to burn at least two hundred watts. "It seems to me," she said pointedly, "that you haven't started dating again. Am I keeping you out of action?" She figured that she had to be. He was spending his weekends, when he wasn't on duty, around her.

"You are not keeping me out of action." He was still smiling. "I haven't been meeting anyone lately that I feel like dating." He saw the devilish look on her face before his own words registered in his head. When they did, he knew where she was going to go with this, just as he knew she had him stymied. The imp had neatly set him up...

Angie confronted Sonny with the beginnings of a smug-alecky smile. She did try hard to keep it in check. "As long as I'm going to sign up, I don't see why you shouldn't sign up with me. In fact, if you don't, I'm not going through with it." She was proud of herself for turning the tables on him, especially since it was for his own good.

Sonny stuck ten fingers into his hair. "No..." He shook his head. "Absolutely not!"

"Didn't you say this was the nineties? Didn't you say the bar scene was passé? And didn't you say the personals were too impersonal? If you're not meeting anyone that you feel like dating, why should you object?"

Sonny's hand lifted, and fell, returning to the counter. He liked it much better when he was running the show. "Look, I'm not the one with a problem..."

Angie leaned intently toward him. "Are you saying that there's something wrong with me? Are you saying that I couldn't attract a man if I wanted one?"

Sonny rolled his blue eyes. "That's not what I mean, and you know it. I think you're bright and pretty. Just about any man would trip over his own feet to get to you. You even know how to be charming, though you haven't been wasting any of it on me."

Angie playfully widened her big brown eyes. "Was there a compliment in there? I want to be sure I didn't miss it."

Sonny rubbed the bridge of his nose. She was getting him exasperated. "All this banter is very cute, but the bottom line is..."

"The bottom line is—" Angie emphasized each word "—*you don't have the guts to sign up.*" She gave him a double-dare kind of look. "You're sure anxious for me to put myself on the line, but you're not willing to stick your neck out."

He was no longer just exasperated. He had arrived at the end of his rope. "I'm trying to do right by you, and you keep turning me into a heavy." Then again, maybe he was asking her to stick her neck out. What kind of a check did the agency do on the guys that were going to want to take her out? "All right," he said abruptly. "I'll sign up."

Rotating in his stool, Sonny stretched to his feet, took her hand and jerked her up. He reasoned that it was a good idea for him to get a sense of how the agency worked—just as it was a good idea to keep his eye on her instead of turning her loose.

"What made you change your mind?" Angie asked as Sonny hurried her back out into the crisp air.

"You talked me into it." The more he thought about it, the more convinced he became that she was too vulnerable and naive to be on her own. He should have considered that right at the start. Fortunately, it wasn't too late.

"I did?" Angie looked at Sonny, bewildered while he rushed her along the way. Was he up to something?

She was a little out of breath by the time they stopped short in front of the reception desk inside Video Magic Dating Service.

The receptionist was typing on a computer keyboard. She raised her long, crimson fingernails from the keys. "Can I help?"

Sonny did the honors. "We'd both like to sign up."

"Great," gushed the receptionist, smiling and keeping her gaze on Sonny. Close to Sonny in age, she made it clear by her expression that she didn't think he needed any help finding himself a woman.

Angie took in the scene, trying to garner Sonny's reaction. Best she could tell, he was taking the receptionist's flirtatiousness casually. Angie looked down at the carpet beneath her flat-heeled leather boots, and then took note of her own hands. She hated her fingers. They were short and stubby, and she kept her nails cut to the pink. She didn't want to chance scratching Melissa or Lindsay.

Sonny glanced at the nameplate on the desk. "Before we do sign up, Joan" Sonny smiled "I'd like to understand a little bit about the way the agency operates. How much of a background check do you do on the people you put together?"

"As you'll see from the forms we ask you to fill out, we're very detailed." Joan opened one of her desk drawers and lifted out two stapled sets of forms.

Sonny accepted both sets. "How do you know that what I put down is the truth? I could be married, and looking to cheat on my wife... Or I could be an escaped convict for that matter..."

Joan laughed, then realized Sonny wasn't trying to be amusing. "We do verify the information you give us."

Sonny wasn't accepting the answer at face value. "Just how do you do that?"

Joan didn't seem to find it unusual to be questioned about the agency's operation. Angie thought that Sonny was being too intense.

"To begin with," Joan replied, smiling, "we call and verify your employment..."

"What if I asked you not to do that?" Sonny questioned. "I might want to keep my private life private."

Joan tipped her head, sending her long blond hair off one shoulder. "We're very discreet."

Sonny ticked off his next question. "Is that the only verification you do?"

Joan shook her head, and rolled her bottom lip. Her lipstick was coral red, and glossy as though it had been just applied. "No, we also call your home number and we check your character references. We do ask that you list two on the form."

Sonny jumped on the last of Joan's responses. "Just two?"

Angie decided to call an end to Sonny's question-and-answer session. He was acting as if he were on duty. "Sonny, I think two character references is more than enough."

Joan took the reprieve as an opportunity to move the process along. "We have rooms in the back where you can fill these out, but there's only one room available at the moment. Who would like to start first?"

"If there are two chairs in there, we can fill them out together," Sonny responded. "We don't have any secrets from each other." Sonny spared Angie a glance. "You don't mind, do you?"

Angie shrugged. She couldn't think of any reason to mind.

"Brother and sister?" Joan asked, taking a guess as she came out from behind her desk.

"Brother-in-law and sister-in-law." Sonny set the record straight. "Angie was married to my brother. He passed away a while ago."

Joan made the requisite condolences. Angie and Sonny nodded.

Joan started down the hall, leading the way. She was tall and very trim with excellent posture. She moved with just the hint of a wiggle. Sonny matched her stride with his easy spring. Bringing up the rear, Angie considered swinging her hips a little. She didn't, though she could have used the practice. Instead, Angie stuck out her tongue—a sophomoric treat for no one in particular.

The glazed ceramic-tiled hallway was clear. Whatever was going on, was going on behind the closed doors they passed.

"Here we are," Joan said, finding an empty room. All three stepped in. "Bring the forms up to me after you've finished, and then we'll have one of our cameramen work up your videos. Let me see if I can round up another chair. There should be a free one in one of the back offices."

"I'll give you a hand," Sonny said, lickity-split.

Angie took off her loden toggle-coat and hung it on a hanger in an open closet. Then she sat down at a varnished oak table in the one leather swivel chair. She glanced at the double set of forms that Sonny had left on the table. She thought of giving herself a head start before Sonny came back in the room. She wanted to get this over with.

Angie was toying with one of the available pencils when Sonny returned. He was cockily one-handing another swivel chair.

Joan smiled approvingly at Sonny, then closed the door behind her on her way out.

Angie noted Sonny's smug male grin as he set the chair in place across from her. "It looks to me like you can skip right ahead to the front of the class," she said. She felt cross with him for some reason that mystified her. It was something other than his having talked her into coming here.

Sonny flashed Angie a wide-eyed look—that blue-eyed people do so well.

"What are you riled about?"

"Me?" Angie shrugged. "I'm not riled."

"You could have fooled me." He leaned back, his arm resting carelessly over the side of his chair.

Angie sugarcoated a half smile. "Let's just get these things filled out." She slid him a set of forms.

"I hope you're in a better mood for the camera," Sonny quipped.

Angie didn't deem it necessary to reply. In the ensuing silence, they both began to pencil in their forms. "I can't seem to concentrate," Angie said finally. "What do you say we do this another day?"

Sonny put his pencil down. "What's wrong?" he asked, knowing the answer. He'd battled her into this, and she was still rebelling.

"Well . . ." Angie began haltingly, looking for an excuse. "*I'm* wrong. That's what's wrong. I didn't dress right. I really should come back another day."

Sonny got up and came around the table. "Stand up and let me look at you again." He took her hands and tugged her to her feet.

Angie complied without protest. Sonny let go of her hands and took a step back to give her a masculine appraisal.

She was wearing a long gray wool skirt with a brown leather belt around her narrow waist, a simple white cotton turtleneck and gold hoop earrings. Her olive-toned complexion still held the flush of outdoors. Now that he was thinking about it, he realized he'd never seen more unusual eyes than hers. A russet rim edged her irises, intensifying the flecks of gold and copper. Her lashes were dark and thick even without mascara. He could see that she was working at toughing out his examination. She had an I-can-take-it expression on her face.

"You look the way you're supposed to look. You look like you." It was the highest compliment he could think of.

"Oh, that's great!" Angie groaned, deciding she really should have put more thought into her appearance.

"Who do you want to look like?" He thought she was a knockout in her own unique way. He didn't know why he found it so hard to just tell her.

"I wouldn't mind looking like *Joan.*" She smiled teasingly into his serious eyes. "I didn't see that you minded looking *at* Joan, either."

"That was just a little friendliness..." He broke off and grinned. "You know how we men are... We've been programmed to act studly."

"Well, what the heck..." Angie sat back down. "I'm glad that you've already found someone that you'd like to take out. Now maybe you'll stop pestering me."

"I'm not interested in dating Joan. She's not my type, and I'm not going to stop pestering you until you have a social life." He gave her a 'so-there' look.

Curious about the first half of his remark, Angie began a discussion. "If she's not your type, what is your type?" She'd known him more than half her life. She was even aware of some of his teenage crushes— after all, she and Rick had gone together off and on since they were teens. In the past few years, he'd brought a number of women to their apartment, accepting dinner invitations and the like. She'd never given much thought to the women he dated.

Sonny smiled. "If you're a good girl and you fill out your form, I'll let you read mine. Is that a deal?"

Angie squinted up at him. "You are smooth, Sonny, I'll give you that."

"I'll take it." He went around the table to his seat, his smile turning into a grin. He didn't know how he'd done it, but he had kept her from bolting.

The first page of the form was a breeze, dealing with their personal statistics.

"Are you up to the tricky questions yet?" Angie asked, paused on page two.

"Uh-huh," Sonny grumbled, also paused. He couldn't believe all he was putting up with to help her out... It wasn't a thrill for him to have to probe himself.

Angie ran her fingers through her curly hair. She'd had it cut to just below her shoulders. "I just can't think of what would be a perfect way to spend a date."

Sonny watched a tiny dimple take shape at the side of her mouth while she chewed the corner of her bottom lip. He knew she was itching for another excuse to blow this whole thing off.

"Let's talk it out," he suggested.

Angie countered, "Let me hear what would be a best date for you. Maybe it will give me an idea. I've forgotten all about dating. I haven't had that much experience with dating to begin with. I don't think I want to do the same things now that I wanted to do when I was a teen. I told you this was a mistake." She needed to take a breath after that mouthful.

"You told me how badly you feel that you haven't been seeing much of the couples that you and Rick used to hang out with. The world is made up of pairs... that's the way it is."

Angie sighed. He was right about that. "I don't know how men and women are supposed to behave at a dating level."

Sonny thought for a second. "I know I prefer that the women I take out behave like themselves. I'd want to meet *her*, not who she *thinks* she should be. If it's right, she should want to know me for who I really am. I've been around enough women who like to play games."

Angie was listening earnestly. "How will you know when it's right?"

Sonny considered her question. "I guess I'm hoping that I'll feel a bomb going off inside of me. How did you feel when you first started going out with Rick?"

Angie's smile came easy. It felt so good to be able to talk about Rick. She found she could do that with Sonny. Her family, even her friends, avoided even saying his name in her presence. "Mostly, I felt like I couldn't catch my breath, and the whole world had become electrified. You've never felt that way?"

"In spurts." His eyes turned intentionally sexy to underline his point. "But not long enough to make it feel right."

Angie groaned. "Be serious." She looked down at the form and sighted one of the questions coming up. "What qualities are you looking for?"

Sonny ran the knuckle of his thumb across his mouth. "Well, I'd like her to be hot, but not in a cheap way. She'd have to be sensitive and funny—someone who might every once in a while do something off-the-wall. She'd have to be able to take teasing, and give it back as good as she got. She'd have to know how to listen, and when to complain, because I do occasionally need to be whipped into shape—not literally, of course." He winked.

Angie laughed. "I wasn't taking that part literally."

Sonny set his joshing aside. "She'd have to be my best friend. I think that's the most important part of all."

Angie pushed back into her seat, relaxing for the first time since she'd sat down. "Boy, is that good... Can I copy off of you?"

"Sure." Suddenly, he wasn't relaxed. The woman he'd been seeing in his mind's eye seemed to be very much like the woman who was sitting across from him. Only, she wasn't the one he wanted to have designs on...

"Come on, let's get this over with," he mumbled.

Angie picked up her pencil and went back to work. She started thinking about the social life she didn't have, and all the married friends that she no longer saw as couples. Maybe it was time for her to figure out how to date. It didn't have to be a big deal. She knew she was never going to fall in love again. But there might be someone out there who would be interested in her companionship.

Angie contemplated Sonny, who had his head down. He was everything a woman would want in a man. He was strong, sensitive, emotional and the quintessential hunk, to boot. It was hard to believe that he was having any trouble finding the right woman. He could sweep just about any woman off her feet with his smile.

Unexpectedly, Angie's mouth went dry, and her heart was pounding. She didn't know how her thoughts about Sonny had led in such a strange direction. She had no idea what to make of it!

Chapter Three

Frankie pitched forward in his seat. "I'm telling you, Sonny, the Rangers are going to take the Cup this year. They've traded for the kind of pistols they've needed."

Sonny took it upon himself as his moral duty to support his own favorite hockey team. "I'm telling you, Frankie, the Islanders are getting it back together, and there's no pistol that's going to penetrate the brick wall they're developing in front of the cage."

"Stop talking sports," Lisa interrupted, coming into Angie's living room. "She'll be out in two seconds. I want you both to give her your full attention."

"How is she, Lisa?" Frankie asked. He'd stopped by to check her out himself, as Teddy had earlier. Nancy had just left with Melissa and Lindsay. She was baby-sitting the girls overnight at her place.

Lisa grinned. "Bucking like crazy. She's been cursing Sonny sideways, backwards, and front. If she could, she'd call off this date for tonight, but she realizes it's too late."

Sonny laughed. "What do you think my chances are of getting her there in one piece?"

"Slim to nil," Frankie joked, then got serious. "No one told me where the two of you are going to be meeting your dates."

"The Rendezvous on East Seventy-ninth," Sonny answered.

Frankie nodded. "Sonny, don't let her go off alone with this guy. She may not be able to handle herself if he's a smooth operator."

"Why do you think I insisted we double-date?" Sonny's tone was knowing. "I'm sticking to her like a cheap suit."

They all heard Angie's footsteps coming down the hall, and that ended the conversation.

"Moppet..." Frankie exclaimed, getting to his feet. "You look terrific."

Angie self-consciously primped.

Sonny admired her from his seat. She was gorgeous and classy. He couldn't recall ever appreciating *classy* as much as he appreciated it on her.

Angie stuck her hands into the slash pockets that were detailed with brass military buttons at her hips. "Lisa feels I should wear something that shows more skin..."

Sonny's eyes roamed up from her black pumps, shiny nude nylons, the zip-front dress with its braided neck, short sleeves and epaulet shoulders. Then his eyes panned back down to her dynamite legs. The dress ended circumspectly just below her knees, but he wondered how high it would hike up when she sat. He thought of suggesting a trial run, and he would have, but he knew she'd only call him a pain in the neck. Instead, he mollified himself knowing that there was going to be a table between her and her date's gaze. And if the guy looked too hungry, he'd punch his lights out.

He wagged his eyebrows up and down for her. "It works for me. Any more skin and you'll have the guy foaming at the mouth."

Angie responded with a perky grin. She was getting back some of her nerve. "Get up, Sonny. Let me look you over."

He obliged, giving her a go at him. She took her time checking out his blue suit, white dress shirt and navy tie. Impatiently taking his car keys from the pocket of his pleated trousers, he tossed them from hand to hand a few times. "Well?" he asked finally, and was disappointed when it was Lisa who answered.

"She'll be putty in your hands, Sonny." Lisa winked.

Angie drew a mental picture that made her feel heated and oddly annoyed. "You should have gotten your hair trimmed. It's a little long in the back." Angie disagreed with herself even as she made the assessment. She didn't know why she'd said it.

"His hair isn't too long," Lisa said.

Sonny rolled with the punch, though he made a note to himself to make some time to get his hair cut. "I like to give them something to wrap their fingers in."

Frankie exchanged a man-to-man look with Sonny. "You two had better get going. Lisa and I will lock up."

Giving Sonny an unwarranted cold shoulder as she turned, Angie picked up a small black leather purse with a gold-link shoulder strap. She hadn't liked his quip to Frankie, though she didn't know what there was about it that had bothered her. She was aware he was just joking the way that guys joke with each other.

Lisa halted her sister's progress. "Wait a minute, your jacket." Running back into the bedroom, Lisa got the long wool jacket that matched Angie's dress.

Sonny went to help her on with it, but Angie grabbed at it before he got to it. "Are you going to be warm enough?" he asked, putting his blue topcoat on.

"We're only going in and out of the car," Angie answered as they walked outside. A coat over her jacket would have been too bulky. The jacket was part of her look.

Sonny turned the heat up in his four-year-old hatchback, even though it was too hot for him.

After a while, he turned his head her way. Her reddish-brown hair had a ruffled look. She had the side facing him pulled back with a gold-plated comb. Some strands had escaped to curl in front of her ear.

"Nervous?" he asked.

"No." Angie shook her head, then admitted, "Yes, and I hate you for talking me into this."

Sonny strung his right hand across the back of her seat and squeezed her shoulder. Angie tilted her face toward him. "I don't really hate you."

"I know." Sonny smiled and continued to drive one-handed. "I can drive somewhere else. We can ditch them both, kick back and just have a good time." He made the suggestion off-the-cuff, but he couldn't have said the idea wasn't appealing. He wasn't particularly in the mood to perform the rituals of the dating game.

"Where would we go?" Angie played along.

"Siouxsie and the Banshees are opening tonight at a club in Nassau."

"Hmm..." She'd never heard of the group. Angie smiled to herself at the difference six years in age could make. "Won't they be sold out?"

"All I'd have to do is flash my badge. Of course, that might not get us seats, but it should get us in the door." He stroked her arm without thinking. "One seat, and you can sit on my lap."

Angie's cheeks flushed at the thought. Sonny felt a vibration that he would have recognized if he'd chosen to recognize it. He did remove his hand from around her, and brought it back to the wheel where he decided to keep himself occupied. His psyche didn't seem to be aware that his mind had placed her off-limits.

For a moment, Angie felt a sense of abandonment as Sonny removed his arm, but she pushed the feeling aside. It was a dumb feeling, at best. "Well, shoot," she grinned. "I've never heard of that group, anyway. Do you want me to start looking for a parking space?'' She could see by the street they'd just passed that they were getting close to their destination. She knew the neighborhood where they were headed though she'd never been to The Rendezvous.

''There's a garage up the street.'' He found it hard to imagine that she'd never heard of Siouxsie and the Banshees. He decided he'd bring her their latest album.

Angie took the comb from her hair, brushed it with her fingers, then resecured it. She was getting all nervous again, thinking of the evening ahead.

Sonny hung a right into the garage, got a ticket and was told there was available parking on the third level up. He expertly maneuvered his car up the hollow, winding, cavernous turns, and found a spot.

''Is my lipstick still on?'' Angie asked, stepping out of the car as Sonny held her door open.

He checked her face under the illumination of the low-intensity floodlights overhead. There was a long pause during which he forgot her question, though his eyes were on her mouth. Was this guy they were meeting going to find an opportunity to kiss her goodnight? Not if he had any say in the matter, Sonny decided. Maybe after a third date... Then again, maybe not even then. There wasn't any rush.

Angie smiled cutely. ''Well...is my lipstick still on?''

''Yes,'' Sonny answered brusquely. The shade she used was too pale a pink for him to be sure. He did know that she didn't need any improving.

Angie looked at Sonny closely. ''You don't have to bite my head off.''

"I'm sorry." He mellowed his tone. "I didn't mean to."

"What's wrong?" She was concentrating on his unexpected attitude.

"Nothing . . . Have you ever felt bothered and restless without knowing why?" It was the closest he could come to an explanation. He didn't know what had gotten into him.

"I guess," Angie conceded. "Maybe you're just nervous about this date."

Sonny shrugged.

"I hope I recognize him." Angie puckered her lips as they started to cross toward the elevator. "Right now, I can't remember what he looks like." She raised her wrist to her face. "I think my perfume's evaporated."

"It hasn't." Sonny mimicked a few staggering steps. Her perfume did reach him, but it wasn't overpowering. He liked whatever it was she was using. "Listen to me, though . . ." He stopped walking. "If you want to call this evening short at any point, just signal me. Okay?"

Angie grew thoughtful. "But what if I want to cut it short and you're having a great time? This might be the girl of you dreams."

"She isn't." Sonny smiled.

Angie gave a teasing smirk. "How can you know that? You haven't met her yet."

Sonny shrugged and bantered, "I've got a gut instinct, and my instincts haven't failed me yet, even though my gut's taken more than one beating."

She was aware he was making a reference to his vocation. She'd bet his gut had taken a number of beatings, and she felt chilled thinking about it. "You've got to have a positive attitude."

He was monitoring her expression. "Do you have a positive attitude?"

She didn't think to lie. "I don't expect to fall in love again. I'm also not thrilled about setting myself up to be rejected. I'm going to be boring. I just know it."

Sonny smiled easily. "You couldn't be boring if you tried." They were standing still facing each other with less than a foot of concrete floor between them.

She contemplated pressing him to elaborate, not that she would have believed him. "I didn't mean what I said about your hair being too long. It isn't too long. I was just being cranky." She suddenly wondered how it would be to wind her fingers into his thick hair. Shock followed that thought, making her look for something else to say. "What kind of signal should I give you if I want to leave early?"

He scratched his plan to get a haircut within the next few days. "How about if you just pull on your earlobe?" He demonstrated. The small clip-on earring she was wearing fell into his palm. He put it back on for her. She readjusted it for herself, her elbows creating more space between them.

He came up with a suggestion from her action. "That's how we'll do it. You take your earring off, then put it back on. I'll have us out of there in nothing flat."

Angie grinned. "I'm going to have a good time." Even if she had to fake it, she was not going to mess up his opportunity of possibly meeting Ms. Right.

Sonny didn't have any trouble reading what was going on in her head, but he didn't argue. He studied her straightforwardly. "You're beautiful," he said without generating any doubts for himself over protocol.

"I'm just okay-looking." Angie chuckled. "But thanks for the brotherly devotion."

He hadn't been thinking like a brother. Her reminder of his status made him frown.

Shoulder to shoulder they began walking. They didn't say anything to each other in the elevator, or even when they were out on the street.

A snazzy-looking guy outfitted in a forties-style zoot suit and wide tie was standing in front of the door of The Rendezvous. He had a clipboard in one hand. It was still too early for a line to form.

"See the guy with the clipboard?" Sonny spoke in an aside. "In an hour or so when they put the red velvet rope up, he'll start picking and choosing who gets in."

"Really?" She'd heard of places like this, where people were judged before being allowed admittance. She and Rick had stuck to the suburbs on their nights out on the town.

"I think they do it just to promote New York nightlife's mystique."

Angie tried not to look intimidated.

Sonny led her inside without ritual. He helped her off with her jacket and checked it with his coat.

The club was dark inside. The walls were green and hung with fake Rembrandts and the like.

"Have you been here before?" Angie asked.

Sonny nodded, and smiled at her look of awe.

They'd decided, when the plans were made, to meet their dates at the bar. It wasn't as crowded now as it would be later. Between eight and ten on Fridays, people came from work to dine, or just have a drink or two before boarding a train to the suburbs.

The bar itself was dark wood. Against the opposite wall, there was a mahogany drink rail. Around them, gilt-rimmed brocade sofas invited respite. Sonny watched Angie gazing around. He was thinking about her concern about being rejected by the guy she was going to meet—not that it could happen. The guy would have to be an idiot.

"He's coming our way," Angie whispered, having spotted her date just moments after he'd spotted her.

He reached them with a pilsner glass of beer in one hand. "Angie?" He had a look of pleasant surprise on his face.

"Chad..." Angie smiled.

Sonny stood to the side. Chad had seen her video. What was he so astonished about?

"Hi," Angie said a little breathlessly.

"Hi," Chad replied, giving her a once-over.

Sonny was doing his own checking, taking the part of devil's advocate. He had seen the guy's picture—not the video, but a snapshot. He'd examined it as intently as he would have a wanted poster. Sonny had to admit the guy, in person, was okay in the looks department, and clean-cut enough. He was wearing a light gray suit with a white shirt opened at his neck. He was slim and fairly tall. He had dirty-blond hair, wide-apart hazel eyes that were perhaps a bit flinty, and an off-center, kind of smirky smile that was something like the one Bruce Willis had made famous. Did women have great sex with guys named Chad?

"This is my brother-in-law, Sonny DeFranco," Angie introduced, looking flushed and nervously excited. "Sonny, this is Chad Brinker."

"Sonny," Chad said.

"Chad," Sonny acknowledged.

They shook hands. Sonny was interrupted by a tap on his shoulder. He turned into it. "Raine?" Sonny smiled appropriately.

"I didn't have any trouble picking you out." Raine smiled back. She had dark hair down to the middle of her back, eight inches of skirt, high-topped logo sneakers and a black cotton, unstructured, guy-jacket opened over a simple white silk blouse.

Angie felt old suddenly—old and envious—and way out of her league. Her own dress, she decided, was too structured. Raine would no doubt know Siouxsie and The Banshees.

Sonny minded his manners. "Raine, this is my sister-in-law, Angie DeFranco and Chad . . . uh . . ."

"Brinker," Chad filled in.

Angie studied Chad, and then Sonny. She was examining the effect Raine was having on them. As far as she could tell, they were both taking the twenty-something woman in stride. It had to be a result of practice on both their parts. Raine was very pretty.

"Angie," Chad said, "would you like to have a drink at the bar first, or should we go to our table?"

Angie didn't want to be the one to make the decision for the four of them. She looked to Sonny.

"I don't know about the rest of you," Raine said, "but I'm starved. I don't usually eat during the day. I save all my calories for dinner."

The decision having been made, Chad put his arm around Angie's waist and propelled her to the stairs leading to the dining area on the second floor.

Sonny didn't see the need for Chad to insinuate such a determined grip on her. Sonny appraised Chad from the rear as he followed along with Raine. He was kind of hoping to spot some balding, but he didn't.

Chad, assuming the role of host with a flourish, spoke to the maître d' and got them to their reserved table.

He was ostentatious, Sonny decided.

"I've never been out on a date with a detective before," Raine remarked after they'd taken their seats.

"Really?" Sonny responded briefly. He was watching Chad whisper something into Angie's ear that brought a blush to her cheeks and a smile to her lips. Chad obviously didn't believe in wasting any time when he had "making time" on his mind.

Raine opened her menu.

Chad shared his menu with Angie. The two had their heads together.

Sonny looked at Raine to give himself a different focus. "You're in advertising, right?"

"Yes." Raine gave Sonny an uncertain smile. "I'm a secretary."

"It must be a fascinating atmosphere." Angie joined the conversation, crossing her legs under the table to give Chad more room. His knee had been accidentally hitting up against her thigh.

"What do you do?" Raine asked, being friendly.

"I'm home with my girls, but I'm hoping to go back to work when they're both in school. I kept records for an auto dealership before I was married, and for some time afterward. We thought we should have a nest egg before we had children."

"Being home with kids is a very important job," Chad said, championing her.

Sonny scowled. Angie didn't need anyone to speak up for her. If she did, wasn't he the one who knew her best?

Their waitress arrived in a tiny black skirt with long blond hair dribbling over her shoulders.

"Would you like something from the bar?" she asked.

"Why don't we get a bottle of champagne?" Chad suggested. "Unless you'd rather have something else?" He looked at Angie.

Sonny noted that Chad's Bruce-Willis grin was in high gear.

"It's been ages since I've had champagne," Angie answered, twisting a little in her seat. Chad's knees seemed to need more room than she'd already given him. "Raine, is that okay with you?"

"Sure," Raine replied, nonchalant.

Sonny eyed Raine. She was a nice kid, and good-looking. He tried to get his mind on her.

"Is this one okay?" Chad asked, pointing out to Sonny the most expensive champagne on the list.

Sonny nodded, and thanked his lucky stars that he'd just paid his credit card bills. He had the feeling that the cash he had in his wallet was not going to be enough to cover this evening's tab.

Sonny centered himself on Raine after the waitress walked off. She was studying her menu again. "What looks good to you?" he asked, reviving his smile.

Raine smiled back. "I've had the halibut here before, and it's really quite good. I usually order fish when I'm out."

"I'm partial to fish myself, when I'm out," Sonny said.

Raine laughed softly. "I guess that's one of the reasons that Video Magic matched us up."

"Could be." Sonny shifted a glance to Angie. "What are you going to have, hon?"

Angie might have been surprised by Sonny's use of that endearment if she hadn't just almost tipped off the side of her seat. She'd been scooting to the edge still trying to avoid Chad's knee.

"Are the legs unsteady on your chair?" Sonny asked, ever-observant.

Angie shook her head, and straightened herself out. She knew her cheeks had reddened.

Their waitress returned just then with champagne glasses. She was accompanied by a busboy bringing along the bottle of champagne chilling in an ice bucket set on a tripod stand.

The busboy, who was too old to be considered a boy, wrapped the bottle in a white cloth and popped the cork with aplomb.

To Sonny's irritation, Chad was offered the rite of approving the first taste.

Chad made a show of swirling a sip in his mouth before swallowing. "Fine," he said with savoir faire.

They were each served a full glass. The waitress took her order pad out from the front pocket of her apron. "Would you like to order dinner now, or shall I come back?"

"I'm ready, and starving if everyone else is," Raine answered.

"I know what I'm having," Angie said, but then deferred to Chad.

"I'm set." Chad smiled. Sonny nodded.

Raine ordered the halibut. Sonny ordered cinnamon-cooked shrimp. Angie requested the sliced lamb on a bed of rice pilaf. Chad copied Angie's order right down to the mushrooms she'd asked for on the side.

Was there anything beyond this guy? Sonny wondered.

The food was good, and they all commented on it, making chitchat as they ate. Angie had finished two glasses of champagne—the second one at Chad's insistence.

"I'd love to read one of your books," Angie told Chad. A little light-headed, she was becoming less aware of the occasional rub of his knee.

"Me, too," Raine added. She'd been enthused at finding out during dinner that Chad was a writer.

Sonny swallowed the last of his third glass of champagne. He wrote travel books... Big deal!

Chad came up with a brilliant suggestion. "I'm sure I have a book in my car." He was speaking directly to Angie. "Why don't you and I go for a ride? I'll give you the book, and you can pass it on to Raine."

"I'm going to have to object to that," Sonny interjected before Angie had the chance to speak.

Chad was immediately annoyed. "What exactly are you objecting to?" Sonny sat indolently in his seat. "I may be off duty, but I still live by the book. You're going to have to wait at least an hour without drinking before getting behind the wheel."

Chad was at a loss.

"I have an idea." Sonny straightened up. "We'll all take a walk to your car. You can give Angie the book, then we'll come back in and dance."

"Well..." Chad said.

Raine looked over at Angie. "I'm going to run into the ladies' room. Would you like to join me?"

Angie got to her feet. "We'll be right back," she said, and the two women left.

Sonny caught the waitress's eye, and got their check. Chad pulled his credit card from his wallet. "Just give me the cash for half."

Sonny pulled out his credit card. "Let's do it the other way around." After a glance, Sonny had tallied up that he was cash-shy.

"I need the write-off," Chad insisted. "I diary all my meals out as a business expense."

Sonny tossed Chad a sagacious glare. No wonder he'd been so quick to order an expensive champagne. "I bet the IRS would be thrilled to hear that."

Aggravated, Chad turned to their waitress. "Could you write two checks, and take both cards? Just split the gratuity... Whatever you think."

The waitress agreeably collected both cards. The check was taken care of by the time Angie and Raine returned to the table. "Are we ready to take a walk to Chad's car?" Raine asked. Angie glanced at Sonny, and was immediately attuned to the shift in his mood. In her eyes, he looked fit to kill. She wasn't fooled at all by the fixed way he smiled.

"Sure, let's go," Sonny answered. "Ladies..." He gestured with his hand for the two women to walk ahead, deciding that he didn't want Angie to be at Chad's side. The guy was a little too free and easy with his hands. Not given a choice, Chad promenaded with Sonny. They stopped at the hatcheck counter and got their coats. Sonny laid down a tip that covered all of them.

Chad's shiny red foreign sports car was parked in the same garage as Sonny's modest American-made hatchback. Chad clicked off the alarm and opened the car from the passenger's side. He sat down to release the door to the glove compartment. Sonny was looking in over Chad's shoulder. Sonny saw Chad's "claim to fame." As he'd suspected, there was more than one book in the glove compartment.

Chad smiled over to Angie. "How do you like that? I didn't realize I had more than one of my books in my car. Now, you can each have a copy to keep. Would you like California or London?''

Angie turned to Raine. ''Which one would you like?''

''Never mind the books...'' Sonny halted the conversation. ''Out of the car, Chad. Now!''

Chad's squinty eyes enlarged. ''What's up?''

Angie gripped Sonny's arm, stopping the hand he was just about to use to yank Chad from the car. ''Sonny, what's wrong?''

Chad exited his car and stood uneasily.

''Angie,'' Sonny said calmly, his eyes squarely on Chad. ''I want you and Raine to go to my car.'' He took his keys out of his jacket pocket. ''Take the elevator. The car is on the level right above this one. Aisle B.''

''No.'' Angie wasn't going to budge. ''I want to know what is happening.''

''Please, honey. Don't give me a hard time,'' Sonny pleaded without sparing her even a glance. He wasn't about to take his eyes off Chad.

''Wait a minute,'' Chad said, coming out of his stupor. ''I think I know what's wrong. You saw my gun.'' Starting to grin à la Bruce Willis, Chad went to reach back into his glove compartment. He didn't get very far. In a wink, Sonny pounced, though he did refrain from using deadly force as he pinned Chad with a stranglehold.

''It's a toy,'' Chad sputtered.

''Take it out, Angie,'' Sonny instructed, not loosening his arm at all from around Chad's neck. ''Be careful. Hold the handle and point it down.''

Nervously, Angie did as she was told. Once it was in her hand, she could feel and see that it was a toy. "Sonny," she said, trying to sound soothing, "it's a water pistol."

Sonny let go of Chad.

Chad sagged while he gulped air.

Sonny didn't wait long to interrogate. "What do you do with the gun?"

Chad drew a pained breath. "I keep it around in case I need to scare off a mugger."

"Dumb idea, pal."

"You're a crazy man, DeFranco!"

"Let's see what I come up with when I do some checking on you," Sonny retorted.

"Check all you want!"

"You can expect to deal with me, personally, if I turn something up." Sonny was on the thin edge of his temper.

"I'm getting out of here." Chad hiked to the driver's side of his car.

"Could you give me a lift?" Raine spoke up. She'd been quiet during the entire go-around. Her voice squeaked.

"Sure. Get in," Chad answered not all that graciously.

"Look what you've done!" Angie said heatedly as their dates peeled away.

Sonny didn't have a response.

Angie stamped off toward the elevator. Sonny moved with her, but he kept his distance.

He helped her into his car. She didn't say anything. He turned the key in the ignition. Except for the rattle of the motor, the car stayed silent. After paying his way out of the garage, Sonny drove aimlessly, hoping she'd cool down.

Angie sat aggravated.

He gave her a good amount of time, then he couldn't stand it any longer. "All right... Let's get it over with. Let me have it." He braced himself.

She gave him a penetrating glare. "You want it? I'll let you have it... I don't need to be taken care of. I can take care of myself. I don't care if Frankie and Teddy hired you. I don't care if you volunteered. I'm firing you. Got it?"

Sonny nodded. Words would have been superfluous.

Angie sighed. "Where are we going?"

"I'm just driving." He stole a glance at her. She looked a little less irate.

"Why?" She tried to make eye contact with him.

Sonny kept his focus straight ahead. "I'm not taking you home until you've stopped being mad at me."

"Then you'd better plan on refilling your gas tank."

"I guess I'm lucky this car is cheap on gas," he teased.

"You're impossible." Angie's lips formed the start of a smile.

Sonny caught it, though she wiped it away as fast as she could. "Did you like him?"

"No." She accentuated her response.

Sonny let out a relieved breath.

Angie had more to say. "I liked Raine. She seemed to be someone you should get to know, but you've ruined that."

"I don't think we had anything more in common than the fact that we both like ordering fish out."

"How do you know? You didn't say more than ten words to her."

The light ahead changed to red, and he braked. Then Sonny did what seemed to come quite naturally. He put his right hand out, drew Angie close and placed what was meant to be a sweet kiss on her mouth. It got to be a little longer and more complicated on contact.

Angie yanked back after she'd begun to contribute. "What are you doing?" Her pulse was jumping. Her fingers were in his hair. She put her misbehaving hand on her lap.

"Apologizing," Sonny answered, wondering if that was truly his only motive.

"It didn't feel like an apology kiss." Angie tried to adopt some semblance of calm.

"What did it feel like?" Like an unexpected streak of oncoming headlights through a fog, it came to him that he wouldn't have minded doing it again.

"I don't know..." Angie waved her hand, but the answer wasn't out there for her to grab on to. "Let's just refrain from apologizing to each other that way in the future."

It was a sensible request. "How would you like to go for coffee? We never got to have dessert."

"Okay." Angie adjusted herself into a settled position in her seat. Her pulse was still jumping.

Chapter Four

"What are you up to, Sonny?" Angie squeezed against the wall in her hallway making room for Sonny to enter. He was carrying a rather large carton.

"You'll see." Sonny continued forward with Angie right behind him.

"Uncle Sonny..." Melissa squealed with delight getting up from the floor in front of the TV. Still in her pajamas, she'd been watching Saturday-morning cartoons for the last hour.

"Un-knee..." Lindsay mimicked jumping up and down in her playpen.

Sonny grinned over to Angie as he placed the carton down in the middle of the living room. "Is she trying for Sonny, or Uncle?"

"I think it's a blend," Angie answered, starting to open the carton.

"Hands off." Sonny lightly swiped her hands aside. "This is my surprise, and I'm making the presentation. Turn off the TV, Moonbeam." He addressed Melissa. "You're going to be first."

Four-and-a-half-year-old Melissa went to the TV.

Angie pursed her lips as though she'd just swallowed a glass of lemon juice. "Sonny, I've told you to stop buying them toys. By the time they get around to examining half the things you've already got them, they'll be married."

"These are not toys," Sonny responded with contrived briskness. "You'd better get that look off your face before it freezes that way."

Angie adjusted her expression, making a production of it. She knew he'd grin.

He didn't disappoint her.

"I want to see in the box," Melissa said, standing at the ready with the TV turned off.

"Me," Lindsay, eighteen months old, screeched. She'd been chattering for quite some time now, but the only words that were clearly discernible were *me, no, Ma, Issa* for *Melissa,* and now *Un-knee.*

Angie took Lindsay out of the playpen and let her waddle around. Sonny took off his denim jacket and tossed it to the couch. He had a black sweatshirt on underneath, and jeans with a button fly front that Angie noticed because he bent to his knees just then. She would have been embarrassed out of her skin had he caught the direction of her gaze. Fortunately, he didn't.

Angie cleared her throat. "Actually, it would be great if you could take the girls out for an hour or so. I was just getting ready to do some cleaning."

"I am going to take the girls out. I'm taking you out as well. Open your hands, Moonbeam." Sonny spoke the last to Melissa.

Melissa did as requested. While Angie looked on, Sonny strapped elbow pads on her oldest daughter. Reaching back into the carton, Sonny took out knee pads and a helmet. "After we make sure it all fits, Mommy can get you dressed, and then we'll put it all back on when we get where we're going."

Angie stood by, baffled, running her fingers through her hair. She hadn't even combed it yet, let alone put on any makeup. Her outfit was a real winner...red jersey jogging pants that she'd cut off unevenly at her knees after they'd gotten holes in them while she was chasing Lindsay during the baby's crawling stage. Her white polo shirt was permanently stained, but still good enough to wear while she cleaned the apartment. She did not look like a class act.

"Look, Mommy." Melissa showed herself off.

Angie was getting uptight over Sonny's maneuvering. She eyed him after giving Melissa a smile. "I am not letting you teach them to play hockey, if that's what you're up to."

Sonny had already scooped up Lindsay, and was in the process of outfitting her. "Don't be silly." Sonny sent Angie a grin. "They're a little too young yet for hockey."

Angie took a stance with her hands on her hips. "What are you planning to do with them looking like that?"

"Go take a look out the window," was Sonny's answer while he worked on Lindsay.

Angie went to the window. Looking out, she saw Sonny's car parked out front with the largest bicycle she'd ever seen strapped on top. "That's a bicycle..." she said, speaking to him over her shoulder.

"For two," Sonny added. "I have a basket to attach to the front for Lindsay, and there's a seat that goes on back for Melissa."

"You've got to be kidding!" Angie groaned.

"I want to go on a bicycle," Melissa said, doing the best she could to jump up and down. She was hampered by her gear.

"Me...me," Lindsay chanted, standing adorably stiff as a board.

"They are not old enough for this," Angie squawked.

"I'd never take any risks with them," Sonny countered. He took the helmets and pads off the girls, having satisfied himself that everything fit. "You don't want to be overprotective. They'll wind up with all sorts of phobias."

"Your dime-store psychology aside, I told you that I have cleaning to do."

Sonny flicked his blue eyes at her. He was not put off. "I'll help you. We'll all help."

"I have to think about this." Angie gnawed her bottom lip. Was she really overprotective?

Sonny coaxed, "You can think while we clean. Where do you keep the vacuum?"

Angie scrubbed the bathrooms while Sonny vacuumed. Sonny stripped the beds in the girls' room while Angie attended to her bedroom. They met in the hallway. She took the dirty linen from him and went to the washing machine. He got the girls to help him put away their toys.

"Nothing like a little team effort," Sonny smiled when Angie came in to inspect.

"I still don't like this idea of yours," Angie retorted, though she had stopped being all that perturbed. She did, at least, trust him not to place the girls in jeopardy.

"Humor me." Sonny grinned. "I've already got a picnic packed in the car. I had the deli make us sandwiches, and I have a thermos of coffee and a thermos of milk. We'll bicycle first, look at the way the leaves have changed colors and then we'll eat. Do you have a blanket we can take? Oh, and we're going to need some cups. Do you have any plastic mugs?"

Angie put up a restraining hand. "Wait a minute. I haven't agreed to this." At this point, she was rebelling against his take-over manner.

Melissa pooched out her stomach—a clear signal that she was getting ready to whine. "Mommy, I want to go." Melissa's eyes were big and round, the same gray that her father's had been. Both girls had their father's eyes, but their mother's curly maroon-brown hair.

"You're outnumbered, babe." Sonny grinned.

"You don't play fair," Angie grumbled, knowing she'd lost.

Sonny winked. "What can I say? You got me dead-to-rights. Now, get your cute little bottom going. I'll start dressing the girls. Put on jeans and a warm sweater. You don't want to have to wear too heavy a jacket."

Angie sent a saucy sneer his way. "Do you want to tell me what kind of underwear I should put on?" As soon as the question flipped from her mouth, Angie reddened.

"Since you're asking—" Sonny said with a sexy leer "—I'm particularly partial to red lace bikinis, and the kind of bra that opens in the front."

Angie sputtered, shocked by his brashness. Sonny quickly put his hand over her mouth. "I don't think we want the girls to hear what you're about to say."

Angie satisfied herself by biting into the fleshiness of his palm, but it was just in fun. Sonny laughed, but took his hand from her mouth. "How about those mugs? Do you have plastic ones?"

"In the kitchen," Angie answered, bouncing off to her bedroom.

"I'm not wearing a helmet," Angie griped after helping Sonny get the bike down from the top of the car. They were in Van Cortland Park.

"Yes, you are," Sonny returned. "I've got one for you and one for me." He didn't feel that he needed one, but he'd guessed in advance that she'd put up even more of a fuss if he didn't have one for himself.

The girls stood squirming impatiently. "We'll be set to go in a few minutes." Sonny gave each of their helmets a tap. "Angie, get me the screwdriver. It's on the floor of the hatch. There's a small box with screws right next to it." He was checking to see how the back seat for Melissa was going to fit on the bike.

Angie gave him a cockeyed look. "Have you gotten any better with your hands since you tried to fix my dishwasher?"

Sonny laughed. "Oh, sure... Build my confidence, why don't you?"

Angie got him the screwdriver and some screws. She felt badly that she'd knocked him, though he'd taken it lightly. As she assisted him with the back seat and the basket, she made a point of deferring to his judgment. She could see that he knew what he was doing.

"Okay, Moonbeam. You're first." With the kickstand down, Sonny lifted Melissa up and placed her in the back seat. When she was fastened to his liking, Sonny raised his leg over the front bar and stood bracing the bike between his strong thighs. "Angie, put Lindsay in."

"I can't remember the last time I rode a bike," Angie said, sitting Lindsay in the front basket and strapping her in.

Sonny caught her eye. "Don't worry. I'll carry you until you get the hang of it again. But you'd better do your share once you get the rhythm. You'll find you never forgot how to do it. You know, like—"

"I know like what," she said, cutting him off. Blushing, she got on behind him. She gripped the handlebars.

Sonny athletically sprung up on the front seat. "You can wash my mouth out with soap later. Okay?"

Angie butted her head to his back, poking him with her helmet. "Remind me if I forget."

"I don't think you will. I'm sure I'll score some more points by the end of the day."

Angie giggled.

"What are you laughing about?" He turned his head to gaze at her.

"This is kind of fun," Angie admitted, not begrudging him her approval.

"Do you just like giving me a hard time?" He tried to sound aggravated as they began peddling.

Angie knew he was smiling, though she couldn't see it. "I figure that if I take the offensive with you, I can stay *de*fensive. It's the only way I can think of to deal with your harebrained schemes. I bet we're the only two people that Video Magic Dating Service has ever asked not to return."

Now, Sonny decided, was not a good time to let her know that he had another dating scheme in mind.

"Lindsay's asleep and Melissa's almost there," Angie said, after looking back at the girls strapped in the car seats. Sonny had added the seats some time ago to the rear seat of his car.

The excitement had gotten to her daughters, and they'd conked out. Angie was still mentally high. Her body, however, felt tortured.

Sonny finished steering into a tight parking space. "I'll carry them in one at a time."

Angie negated his offer with a shake of her head. "Just carry Melissa. I can manage Lindsay."

Melissa roused herself as best she could while Sonny carried her to the apartment door. "I want to do more."

"Not today." Sonny smiled at her.

Shifting Lindsay to her hip, Angie used her key.

"Today," Melissa murmured.

"Another day." Over Melissa's head, Sonny made eye contact with Angie. "When your mother can handle her share again."

"I was pedaling right to the end," Angie rebutted, lying without any qualm as they walked together to the girls' bedroom.

"In a pig's eye." Sonny grinned. "Believe me, my thighs knew the difference."

"Just admit it," Angie countered. "You are not as macho as you think you are." Damp tendrils fell over her temple, and curls clung to her cheeks.

Sonny thought of the women he'd been with who hated even a single hair being out of place. "One thing's for sure. I am never going to get a swelled head hanging out around you."

Angie nonchalantly shrugged one shoulder at him, and laid Lindsay down in her crib.

Sonny sat Melissa down on her bed. He helped her out of her jacket, then helped Angie take off the baby's jacket and sneakers. She tenderly tucked Lindsay in. Lindsay mewed a little, but didn't wake. Sonny reflected on the many times Rick must have watched Angie taking care of the girls, and his heart hurt for the many times more that his brother would miss.

Angie came over and took off Melissa's sneakers.

"Mommy, I don't want to go to sleep," Melissa grumbled.

"You don't have to sleep if you don't want to," Angie answered smoothly. "But you have to take a rest."

Melissa fought to keep her eyes open. "Uncle Sonny, are you going to stay?"

"Yes," Sonny reassured her. He hadn't completed all he had on his agenda. The balance, however, revolved around Angie, not the girls. He hoped he'd exhausted her enough for her to be malleable.

Melissa got a last wind. "What are we going to do later?"

"We'll see," Angie answered. She didn't want Sonny to feel they were monopolizing all of his time.

"I have an idea," Sonny said. "How about if we make a date to go swimming tomorrow? Would you like that?"

Angie was almost speechless. "Swimming?"

"Indoors," Sonny smiled. "Have you heard of 'Swimming Babies'?"

Angie shook her head.

"It's a new franchise operation. They have a large indoor pool, sandboxes and kiddie rides."

"Mommy, can we?" Melissa begged.

So much for not monopolizing his time. "Okay," Angie agreed, and gave Melissa a kiss.

"Uncle Sonny," Melissa called out as Angie and Sonny started for the door. "Can you bring me my helmet?"

"Sure, Moonbeam."

"Would you like some fresh coffee?" Angie asked when they were in the hallway.

"That sounds good," Sonny said, and they parted. Angie went to the kitchen. Sonny went out the front door to get the helmets from the floor of the car's hatch.

Angie was pouring two cups of coffee when Sonny got to the kitchen.

"What?" he asked, sitting down at the table. The gaze she was giving him was all soft and warm.

"The girls had a wonderful time." She put a cup in front of him. "You must have spent a lot of money renting that bike and buying everything else. Let me, at least, go half with you."

"Indulge me. There aren't any other women in my life that I'd rather spend money on."

Angie sat down opposite him, knowing from his expression that arguing over this wasn't going to get her anywhere. "The point is that there should be some woman in your life."

Sonny knew an opening when he heard one, and this was probably the best one he was going to get. "As a matter of fact, I've made plans to address that issue."

"Really?" Angie was all eyes and ears.

Sonny hauled in a deep breath. "I've signed us up for another dating service."

"Us?" Angie exploded. "Did you say *us?*"

"Just hear me out." He put both his elbows on the table and leaned forward.

"I'm not going to listen." To make her point, Angie covered her ears with her hands.

Sonny gave her a theatrically pathetic look. "Well, I guess you're going to condemn me to bachelorhood."

"That's blackmail," Angie retorted, but she did lower her hands. "I'll listen to you, but I'm not going to agree to take any part in this. No way, Sonny."

Sonny tapped his knuckles on the table. He cocked his head at her, but he didn't say anything.

Angie finally prompted him. "Well? Are you going to tell me, or what?"

Sonny shook his head. "I'm not telling you anything while you've got that clenched look on your face. Give me a little of that sweetness of yours."

She'd agreed to listen, but she didn't have to like it. Angie muttered under her breath.

Sonny interrupted, "Are you almost finished? If you're not, I can wait."

Angie aggressively jutted her chin out, but she was only faking her anger now. She hadn't been that angry to begin with—just agitated.

"That's a little better. " Sonny smiled. Then he got right to it.

"This service doesn't use videos. There aren't even any forms." He gave her a buddy look. "I know how you hate filling out forms."

"Go on." She kept her eyes on him. To his credit, Sonny shifted slightly, nervously.

"It's basically a very simple premise." Sonny paused to take a sip of his coffee. "You went to school dances with Rick when the two of you were teens. This is very much like that."

"A dance?" Angie angled her head. She knew how good he was at dancing her around in a circle. She was determined to stay on her toes.

"Not a big dance," Sonny continued with put-on casualness. "These are not held in any hall."

"You still haven't said exactly what 'these' are. Where are they held?"

Sonny cast a smile in her direction. "Having a conversation with you is more like sparring than talking. All we need is a ring." He squared off to go another round. "Not that I mind it... I just don't have any point of reference. I've never dealt with any other woman the way you make me deal with you."

Angie gave him a comically droll look. "Is that an analysis or a criticism?"

Sonny laughed. "There isn't anything about you that I'd criticize. Don't ever change."

His compliment flustered her. She couldn't think up a comeback.

"Cat got your tongue?" Sonny ribbed her.

She was not going to let him gloat. "Aren't we getting off the subject?"

"Just straying a little."

Angie could feel the high color that tinted her cheeks. "Let's get back to your one-two punch, okay?"

"Here it comes." Sonny leaned back in his chair, tipping the front legs off the linoleum. "I signed us up for a party tonight. It's at an apartment in midtown Manhattan. There should be about twenty to thirty people there, but there's no one-to-one fixing up ahead of time. It all very relaxed. Some eating, some dancing, some conversation..."

"Tonight!" Angie put her face in her hands. "How could you commit me to something like this without giving me any notice?"

"I'm giving you notice. I'm telling you right now."

"I am not going, Sonny..." This idea of his was about as thrilling to her as the thought of going in for root canal work.

Sonny played out his hand. "Do you want to be responsible for throwing the party out of whack? They can't have nineteen to twenty-nine people there. Someone's going to be the odd man out."

"Are you saying that you're going even if I don't go?" She suspected that he was using reverse psychology on her.

"You may not want to meet someone you'd like to date, but I'm definitely in the market for a woman. Of course, I'll probably stand to the side, and be the wallflower there. It will be my fault for messing up the status quo."

"Can I just tell you something?" Angie groaned.

"Sure." Sonny tried not to look as though he knew she was weakening.

"I'm just terrible at small talk," Angie confessed.

"Honey, small talk is easy. You say something about the weather... like wasn't it a great day to be outdoors. He nods, and says, 'Just perfect.' Then you ask a question like, 'Have you been to many of these parties?' If he answers that he has, you excuse yourself, and go on to someone else."

"Why do I do that?" She was getting a headache.

"Because it sounds to me like he's either a hound, or doesn't know what he wants."

"A hound?" Angie knew she'd been out of the dating scene awhile, but hated to appear so naive to Sonny.

"You know, a player—a guy who likes to collect a lot of phone numbers. A smooth-talking date 'em, bed 'em, dump 'em type."

Angie took a gulp of her coffee. "It could be that he just hasn't met the right woman."

"All right. You want to ask him a couple of more questions, ask."

"Why don't I just get to the bottom line, and ask him if he's a hound?" She was trying to be witty. She had to be something, lying down on the mat, taking the count.

"Hounds never tell the truth." His blue eyes gleamed at her with his lazy charm.

"I guess you should know."

"Hey, I'm insulted," Sonny rejoined, not that he'd taken her remark seriously.

"I was only joking." Angie sighed.

"I know." He smiled at her.

Angie sighed again. "I have nothing to wear. Did you think about that?"

Sonny got to his feet and came around the table. "Come on, I'll help you look in your closet."

"Nooooo..." Angie stretched out the word.

Sonny threw out another suggestion. "We can see if we can get someone to watch the girls, and I'll take you shopping. If you don't want me along, I can watch the girls and you can go."

She didn't know what she wanted, or even what kind of outfit to buy. "I could call Lisa. Maybe I can raid her wardrobe. She should be home. She'll bring some stuff over."

"I don't think anything in your sister's wardrobe will be right for you." He understood where she was coming from. She was thinking once again of not being herself. "Why don't you wear that dress you wore when we went to The Rendezvous?"

Angie made a face. "I hate that dress now."

Sonny bent down. He caught her face loosely between his forearms as he steepled his fingers behind her head. He looked into her eyes. "Don't try to be someone else. You're perfect just the way you are."

Angie smiled wanly. "I thought I knew who I was. I was a mother and a wife. I'm still a mother, but that other part of me is missing now. I don't know what that part is supposed to be anymore. I hate the idea of being out there listening to some guy's story, having to tell him mine. Even if he's the nicest guy in the world. It doesn't make sense anyway. I don't want a lover, Sonny. I'm not ready for one. I don't know if I ever will be. Do you really think there's a guy out there who is just looking for companionship? Just a friendly relationship?"

Absolutely not, he thought to himself. Only, she was never going to be ready to get herself a full life if she didn't start getting out.

He summoned one of his easy grins. "Let's compromise. We'll go tonight, but we won't have a good time. How does that sound?"

Angie laughed, then quieted. Sonny could tell there was a change in the cadence of her breathing. He was savvy enough, and experienced enough to know that she was suddenly thinking exactly what he was suddenly thinking. One move...that's all it would take from either of them and they'd be kissing. Only, this wasn't supposed to be happening...

He blew a breath on her temple, ruffling her hair. The last thing he wanted to do was confuse her more than she already was confused. Hell, he didn't even have any straight answers for himself. He wasn't supposed to want to kiss her...

Angie lowered her eyes, but didn't try to move her head outside of Sonny's hold. She stared at the cleft in his chin that was so compellingly masculine. The air between them was humming like the blades of a fan set on its highest speed. Maybe, she did need to concentrate on getting out...

"Mommy," Melissa yelled, standing at her bedroom door. "Did I sleep enough?"

Embarrassed, as though they'd been caught doing something that they shouldn't have been doing, Angie ducked her head. Sonny's arms quickly came away. Sonny rolled from his heels back up to a standing position.

"Yes," Angie answered Melissa. "Check and see if Lindsay is awake." Her voice didn't sound like her own.

Getting to her feet, Angie turned away from Sonny and went to the sink for no particular reason except that she knew she was flushed.

Sonny was relieved that Melissa had interrupted them. It had been sheer gritty discipline on his part that had kept him from acting on his impulse to kiss Angie…the impulse he had even now. "I can take the girls off your hands for a few hours if you'd like. You can play dress-up with Lisa without being bothered."

"You don't mind?" Angie asked over her shoulder without looking directly at him.

"I don't mind." He made a business of examining what was left of the coffee in his cup.

"What time are we supposed to be there tonight?"

"Between eight and eight-thirty."

Angie turned and stared at him. "Why do I let you keep talking me into these things?"

Chapter Five

Angie wriggled out of Lisa's clutches and combed her bangs back down. "Leave my hair alone. I'm not wearing that do-dad."

Lisa pouted. "Rhinestone clasps are very *in,* and I like your hair off your forehead."

Angie let out a long breath. "I don't want my eyebrows to show."

"What's wrong with your eyebrows?"

"I hate my eyebrows. They're too thick."

"Your eyebrows are not too thick." Lisa gave Angie a critical survey. "When Sonny gets here, we'll ask him what he thinks. Shouldn't he be here by now?"

"He's taking the girls over to Nancy's first. They're staying there tonight." Angie put her comb down. "You are not to ask him what he thinks about my eyebrows. Do you hear me, Lisa?"

Lisa teased, "He'll probably be speechless, anyway, once he sees you in this dress."

"Don't you have to get going?" Angie muttered.

"No." Lisa provokingly moved her shoulders up and down. "I'm not leaving until Sonny's at the door. I know you. You'll change if I go."

"I won't," Angie answered airily, but she was contemplating doing just that. She hadn't considered until she'd started trying on Lisa's clothes that Lisa's dresses would be even shorter on her than they were on Lisa. At five foot five, she was three inches taller than Lisa. The black wool sheath with cap sleeves and V-neck was the longest dress Lisa owned. It ended at least three inches above Angie's knees. She'd rejected the silver belt that Lisa usually wore with the dress—it would have brought the hem up even higher.

"What earrings are you going to wear?" Lisa was poking around in her sister's costume jewelry box.

"My small gold hoops, I guess."

Lisa shook her head. "All these earrings of yours have been out of style since the Dark Ages. Wear mine." Lisa took off her chunky gold dangling earrings.

Angie gave them a try, facing the mirror above the dresser in her bedroom. Her closet door with it's full-length mirror was still open.

Lisa smiled. "Perfect... You look hot!"

Angie contradicted. "I look like I'm trying to come off younger than I am." She didn't want to be testy, but she had a stimulating feeling inside of her that was making her nervous.

"You *are* young," Lisa rebutted.

The doorbell rang.

"Put the red lipstick on that I brought you. I'll get the door," Lisa said, running off.

Angie put her own pale pink lipstick on.

"Sonny is here," Lisa called out.

"I'm coming," Angie returned. Her stimulation and nervousness combined into a powerhouse streak of tension.

Lisa regarded Sonny while he regarded Angie. Angie saw Lisa's smug expression, but missed the way she just about brought Sonny to his knees—not that she would have guessed that his heart was pumping crazily.

"I'm going," Lisa said, and hot-footed it to the front door. "Tell her how she looks," she prompted Sonny, before she stepped out.

Sonny put his hands in the pockets of his gray suit pants. His jacket spread open over a black crewneck sweater.

"You look very..." He took one hand out of his pocket and glibly fanned his face. His eyes were unqualifiedly sexy as he gave her a come-hither look. "Wow!"

Angie blushed, acutely discomforted. "Oh, shut up..."

Sonny laughed. "I just got here. How did I strike out with you already?"

He made her grin. "You look very..." She mimicked him by fanning her own face, then said, "Wow, yourself!" She meant it.

Sonny swooped in, and got her around the waist. He didn't bother to try to detonate his urge to be affectionate.

Angie gazed capriciously into his face. "Give me one good reason why you put up with me."

Sonny winked. "Can I get back to you on that?"

Angie gave in to the impulse to touch his hair behind his neck where it reached the collar of his jacket. "Are you going to behave yourself tonight?" Her eyes toyed playfully with his.

Sonny's right hand moved. His fingers spread against her back. "I'm hurt," he said with improvised pathos. "I always behave myself."

Angie wondered what it would be like to rub her cheek against his—not that she'd ever do it. "Sonny, I mean it! You are not to check out any man that might speak to me, if any do. I want you to have a good time. Okay?"

Sonny tipped his head aslant. "Only if you promise that when it's time to leave, you leave with me."

"That makes sense," Angie bantered, "unless I meet someone who lives nearer to me."

Sonny grinned and teased with his eyes. "If you find someone who lives closer to you than three blocks away, I might be willing to discuss it."

Angie smiled engagingly. "I'll promise right now to leave with you if you promise to collect some phone numbers."

"I appreciate your confidence, but I'm hardly irresistible." He thought of the men that would be there, chasing after her—which was the whole point of this.

Unconsciously, Sonny pressed his hand tighter against her back.

Angie turned out of his hold. He was wrong thinking he wasn't irresistible. Sooner or later, he'd meet a woman with the qualities he was looking for. And she'd be happy for him. She'd be very happy...

Raising his arm to check his watch, Sonny wondered to himself how she'd respond if he was to suggest that she change her dress—preferably to something down to her toes and up to her neck. Not that he was thinking possessively, he told himself. He was just being a big brother.

The apartment's address just missed being posh. It would have been an even further stretch to call the building elegant. Still, it had an awning and a sentry—an old man in a visored cap and pale gray uniform. Sonny showed him their invitation and he stepped aside to admit them.

"Before I forget, I spoke to your mother this evening," Angie said as they crossed the lobby filled with frayed velvet couches and black hardwood furniture. "They're both fine. It was eighty degrees in Florida today. They miss everyone, of course. But it was a good move for them."

"I know. They called me right after they spoke to you." Peripherally, Sonny watched Angie's black coat swing as she walked. She'd left it unbuttoned. The dress wasn't tight on her, but it did intentionally cling.

Angie's eyes flickered to Sonny's profile. She noticed the lock of dark hair that had fallen to his temple. She itched to slick it back for him. "They want me to come down in January or February with the girls for a week or so. I may go. I think Lindsay is old enough to travel. I'll go by train, though. I'm terrified of flying."

"There's nothing like Florida in the heart of winter." Sonny pressed for the elevator. "I'm planning to go down and see them myself. I could go down with you." He smiled, picturing them all romping on the beach.

"By then, you may have met someone that you'd rather take down with you." Angie flashed him a directive with her eyes, wanting to remind him of the assignment she'd given him for the evening.

The elevator doors opened, and they stepped in.

Sonny vaulted a bland smile. "You might also meet someone that you'd rather take down to Florida with you and the girls."

Angie sighed inwardly.

Sonny drew a deep breath, and rotated his shoulders, suddenly wrought-up. "Listen, only give your first name tonight unless you meet someone you'd like to give your phone number to."

Angie nodded. "That's a good idea."

"It's the way these parties are run."

The party was on the sixth floor. They heard the sound of the stereo on high the moment they stepped off the elevator.

One of their hostesses met them at the door. She was fluid and sultry with dark straight hair that was parted in the middle and cut just to her shoulders. She wasn't pretty, but she was eye-catching. And she was tall...almost as tall as Sonny, who was five-eleven. She was showing her legs off in her black high heels and a red minidress.

Angie regretted not wearing Lisa's silver belt.

"Hi, I'm Michele." Their hostess tapped the white paper name tag on the front of her dress. "I'll take your coats."

She hung them in a walk-in closet. "Come over to the table and fill out tags. It's a lot easier to remember names that way when you're meeting so many people for the first time. I know I always get embarrassed when I've forgotten someone's name."

Angie and Sonny gazed across the lay of the land. Facing them was the living room. It had been cleared of furniture except for some scattered folding chairs and a row of tables at the far end that displayed a buffet. Angie estimated that there had to be over twenty guests.

There was enthusiastic talk all around them, along with the rocking beat of the music coming from the stereo. One brave couple was dancing. They laughed with each other trying to get their motions to match.

Following Michele, Sonny and Angie hadn't progressed more than halfway across the polished wood floor when they were waylaid by another brunette, her name tag reading "Cheryl." She was delicate and cuddly with shoulder-cut raven hair held to one side with a rhinestone clip. She was dressed in a loose white blouse in the cut of an artist's smock. She wore it over a short dark green skirt, matching opaque tights and Western boots.

"Hi," Cheryl said, munching on a frank in a blanket. "I see you've met Jeff. I'm Mutt . . . Jeff's roommate."

They all grinned at the joke. Angie decided that if she were choosing for Sonny, she'd give her vote to Cheryl over Michele. Each was attractive in her own right, each young enough for him, but Cheryl had more personality.

"I just realized that I never let you introduce yourself." Michele backtracked, setting her gaze on Sonny.

"I'm Sonny, and this is Angie."

"Hi." Angie smiled, thinking she might have liked to use *Angela* tonight—only she'd probably forget to answer if someone called her by her full first name. There was a knock on the front door. Michele looked at Cheryl. "Do you want to do the honors this time?"

Sonny interjected, "Don't worry about us. We can find the tags."

Both their hostesses took off.

The stick-on name tags were in a bowl at one end of the buffet table, along with a paper cup full of ballpoint pens. Sonny took two tags and two pens, handing one each to Angie. They filled out their names. Angie put hers on the front of her dress, and Sonny stuck his to the lapel of his jacket. In a flash they were surrounded by other guests, as if the pasting of name tags signaled they'd been officially inducted.

Sonny was coaxed onto the dance floor by a frothy blonde with a figure to die for.

Angie found herself sequestered with a baby-faced admirer who insisted they stroll over to the opposite end of the long table for a glass of punch.

"I'm glad it hasn't turned cold out yet." Angie made small talk. "The winter can be such a drag." She took a sip from her glass. The liquid was red, sweet and spiked with vodka.

"Uh-huh," Phil agreed, and then began a running monologue. He spoke as quickly as a door-to-door salesman. He didn't have a jacket on. The white collar of his shirt was open, and his red print tie was askew.

Angie nodded every so often, relieved that she didn't have to make any effort. Only, her smile was beginning to make her cheeks hurt, and she wasn't sorry when a "George" materialized and asked her to dance.

On the stereo, "The Sweetest Thing" was playing. Angie didn't know the song. It was slow, and the title was easy enough to figure out. The refrain was repeated at the end of every line.

Gazing over her partner's shoulder as he fitted her into a dance position, Angie scanned the room for Sonny. She saw him in conversation with Cheryl. They were both having something to eat. Angie made herself stop looking his way.

"Perfect day today, wasn't it?" George asked near to Angie's ear.

"Yes." Angie smiled. His hair was curly blond, damp from styling gel. He had a great body, and his features were even. She wouldn't have been surprised if he was a male model. "Have you been to this kind of party before?"

"This is my first," George answered. "But I've tried just about everything else. How about you?"

"I had one date through Video Magic."

"I'm on file with them. Which office did you join?"

"The one on West Fifty-fifth." Angie pivoted in place to George's hip-swaying two step that kept her in a small circle.

"Hey, me, too." George smiled. "What's your number? I'd like to take a look at your tape."

"GX53." Angie didn't see any harm in giving it to him. After all, they'd either burned her tape by now, or recorded over it.

Private amusement playing on her mouth, Angie glanced in the direction that she'd last seen Sonny. He was still there, and still eating, though now he was talking to Michele. She saw him put his half-filled paper plate down to escort Michele out to the dance floor.

The music picked up in beat.

"How about we have something to eat?" George suggested, coming to a halt.

"Okay." Angie looked over at Sonny gyrating as she walked at George's side. She couldn't recall ever seeing Sonny dance before. He was very good and he looked good, too....

Three cassette tapes later, and four hours into the party, Angie had spoken to just about every man there. She'd danced at least once with most—a number of times more with George. Both George and Phil had pressed for her phone number. She'd politely refused while trying hard not to hurt their egos. Neither seemed to take her rejection personally. Passing, Angie decided, the ultimate test of the dating scene.

Sonny listened without enthusiasm to his horoscope being read by a "Felice" who just happened to have brought along a book about the subject. The narrative was about as significant to him as someone threatening to jump from a ground-floor window.

"I'm a real believer in the stars. You can just about figure out everything that is going to happen to you," Felice said.

"I'd rather be surprised," Sonny said with irony.

Angie watched Sonny shoulder his way toward her. Her pulse quickened.

"Dance with me?" Sonny smiled the first real smile of the evening. He'd kept his distance all night. He hadn't wanted to cramp her style. However, he'd made it his business to get into a conversation with a bodybuilder named George that she'd spent a good deal of time with.

Angie pushed forward from the wall she was leaning against. She put down the paper hot-cup filled with lukewarm coffee. "Sure." She smiled back at him.

A reggae beat throbbed as Sonny took Angie into his arms. "How'd you do with the small talk?" he asked, cognizant of how easily they fell into step with each other.

"Weather got to be a bore, so I switched to food. Then, one of the women told me that the way to go was with favorites."

"Favorites?" came Sonny's puzzled response.

Angie tipped her head back. The penny streaks in her reddish-brown hair caught the light. "What's your favorite movie?"

Sonny didn't have to think long. *"Lethal Weapon."*

Angie shook her head. "Bad answer."

"What's a good answer?" He pretended to be serious.

"You're supposed to use a movie that will make a woman think that you're romantic."

"I *am* romantic," Sonny quipped.

Angie teasingly jabbed his back. "I understand that *Casablanca* will score you the highest points, especially if you can recite some of the lines."

"You danced a number of times with George." Sonny changed the topic.

"He's nice . . . and, uh . . . funny." She wanted him to be pleased that he'd arranged for her to be here. "I guess you met George."

"Yes." Sonny drew her body nearer to his. Angie turned her head so that he was no longer able to see her face. Her cheeks had heated. She hadn't expected him to hold her this close.

"You spent a lot of the evening with Cheryl." She took a turn at observation.

Sonny nodded his head. His jaw brushed her hair, and he wondered what shampoo she used that made it so soft.

"Did you get her phone number?" Angie missed a turn and nearly stepped on his toes.

"I got her number." But he couldn't see himself using it—not that there was anything wrong with Cheryl. Maybe, he was getting too tired of the game.

The song ended. Someone pushed a new cassette into the tape deck. The speakers vibrated once again with heavy rock and roll.

"Do you want to get out of here?" Sonny asked.

Angie was quick to consent.

After they'd walked briskly through a cold drizzle, and settled into the car for the ride home, Sonny asked, "Did you have a good time?"

"Yes." Angie smiled winningly as he sent a look her way. "Did you have a good time?"

"Yes." Sonny shrugged.

They chatted back and forth about the people they'd met, only she didn't mention anything more about George. He wanted to ask her specifically about George, but he didn't.

Angie laughed as Sonny talked about his horoscope. She wanted to hear more about Cheryl, but he didn't even bring up her name, and Angie couldn't get herself to ask.

"You don't seem to be tired," Sonny said while Angie fit her key into the door to her garden apartment.

Angie shook her head. "Are you?"

It had to be nearly one a.m. He knew he was still hours away from sleep. Besides, he didn't want to say good-night to her. "I tell you what I am ... I'm still hungry. Why don't we raid your refrigerator and watch some TV?"

"I have leftover lasagna in the freezer. I could put it in the microwave." She didn't want to say good-night to him, either.

Once they'd hung up their coats, Angie kicked off her heels and unscrewed Lisa's dangling earrings. "I'll get the food going." She headed for the kitchen, massaging her earlobes.

Walking into the living room, Sonny took his jacket off and dropped it to one of the chairs. He turned the TV on and flicked the channel selector, hoping to find an old movie that she might like to watch. He knew her favorites were anything with Cary Grant.

He settled on a prerecorded comedy show. It was either that, a horror movie, or music videos, and he was fairly certain that she'd had her fill of music by now.

Angie came in and sat down on the couch, where Sonny was already slouching. She was a full cushion away, sitting stiffly, the way she would have sat in a jet taking off.

Sonny kept his eyes on the screen. "Why don't you make yourself more comfortable? Get undressed. Put a robe on." He made the suggestion off the top of his head, but as soon as the words were out of his mouth, he realized how they sounded.

"I'm fine." Her tone sounded harsh.

Sonny worked at getting himself to relax.

Angie sprung to her feet. "I'm going to check on the lasagna. Do you want to have it here or in the kitchen?"

Sonny shrugged. The TV camera was panning the audience, and they were all laughing. Sonny faked a grin, as if he'd understood the punch line.

Angie manufactured a smile, pretending that she'd also gotten the joke. "This guy is really funny. I'll bring us both a plate in here."

Sonny watched Angie from the rear as she walked out. She'd said George was funny... What was so funny about George? He'd thought the guy was a dud!

Angie returned within minutes carrying two plates of lasagna—a large square for Sonny, a smaller square for herself. His legs were stretched out under the glass coffee table; his hands were behind his head. He was giving a perfect imitation of being at ease. Inwardly, he was wound as tight as a cord of rope knotted to a new roll.

Angie put the plates down on the coffee table. "What would you like to drink?"

Sonny straightened. "I'll get the drinks. What are you having?"

"A soda...and get forks and napkins." Angie watched Sonny walk off. She thought about him being with Cheryl. Was Cheryl really right for him?

Sonny came back with forks, napkins, a beer for himself, a soda for her. He put everything down, then picked the beer back up and chugged a long swig straight from the bottle.

Hoots and loud applause were coming from the TV. Angie tried a smile, but missed. Sitting primly and properly, Angie got busy with her food. Next to her, Sonny kept drinking his beer.

"I thought you were hungry?" she asked, avoiding his eyes.

Sonny put his beer down, lifted his plate and began eating. "So, you liked George?" he asked between bites. Had she given him her phone number?

Angie nodded, her mouth full. She wasn't interested in George. "And you liked Cheryl," she said when she'd swallowed.

"What made you think that?" Sonny raised the bottle of beer to his mouth, having polished off his lasagna in record time.

Angie half chewed a mouthful, and gulped it down. "You took her phone number... Do you want more?"

Sonny shook his head.

"This guy is a riot, isn't he?" Angie tried another unsuccessful smile.

Sonny was not paying attention to the comic's routine, though he was looking at the TV. "Yeah." After chugalugging the last of his beer, he put the bottle down.

"Another beer?" She'd taken to keeping her refrigerator stocked with the brand he preferred. Sonny shook his head again.

Angie put her half-finished lasagna down. She couldn't eat another bite. She was agitated.

"Cheryl is..." she began just as Sonny said, "George..."

They smiled at the way they'd each cut the other off.

"You first," Sonny said.

Angie flicked her hand. "No, you first."

They moved at exactly the same instant. Sonny's mouth found Angie's mouth, and neither had anything more to say. The kiss was wild, superheated, steamy. Sonny was in overdrive. Angie wrapped her arms around his neck, twisting to get closer to Sonny's warmth until he pulled her into his lap. Only the fact that they had to come up for air forced them apart. By then, they'd been at it for a good five minutes.

Angie jumped up as she filled her lungs. "You should not have done that!" Facing off, she gave him her most intimidating glare.

Sonny was trying to get his senses and his body back under control. "You did it, too!"

Angie paced. "I should slap your face."

Her expression made Sonny grin. "You, and who else?"

Angie's mouth opened, shut and opened again. "I don't believe this! You're joking, and this is serious stuff!"

"It always helps to laugh a little." He tried reasoning with her, anything to be spelled from the conversation. He didn't want to talk about what had just happened.

"I don't feel like laughing. My life is all jumbled up!" Angie began pacing again. "I don't know how I feel about anything anymore...except for the kids." She took a deep breath and covered her face with her hands. "Rick's face is not as clear in my mind as it should be, and I'm scared," she said finally.

Sonny started to get up from the couch to take her into his arms, but he vetoed the idea midway. "I think that's part of the healing process," he said softly.

Angie stopped moving and stood facing him, looking small and lost, he thought. "I don't want to be healing... It just doesn't seem fair for me to be healing."

He ached for her. "Healing is part of life, honey. We have to heal."

"I'll tell you what we have to do..." Angie sighed raggedly. "We have to stop spending so much time together... We spend much too much time together. We're leaning on each other, and that's going to get us both into trouble."

"What about tomorrow?" The wheels in his head went round and round as he processed her final statement. Were they leaning on each other for solace? The possibility didn't mesh with his physical reactions. However, he couldn't speak for her.

"What's tomorrow?" She wasn't thinking clearly.

"'Swimming Babies'..." He took his eyes off her face. "I don't want to disappoint the girls."

"Right..." She didn't want to disappoint the girls, either. After tomorrow, she promised herself, she was going to stop seeing him so frequently.

Chapter Six

"I want the red pail," Melissa complained from the back seat of Sonny's car.

"Nooooo!" Lindsay yelled as her sister tried to yank the red pail from her hand.

Angie twisted to face her daughters. "Uncle Sonny can't drive this way. If the two of you don't behave, he's going to turn the car around, and we are not going to 'Swimming Babies.'" Actually, Angie wasn't all that upset that Melissa was acting out. It gave her a focus. She was feeling awkward around Sonny today.

"But Mommy..." Melissa finished off the rest of her sentence by screwing up her face.

Sonny caught Melissa's pout in his rearview mirror. "I'll tell you what, Moonbeam—if they sell any pails there, I'll buy you a red one." He'd had to hunt all over to find pails and shovels for them at this time of the year.

Angie fired annoyed eyes at Sonny. He kept spoiling the two of them. "She picked the yellow one when you brought the pails over."

Sonny smiled what he hoped was his most persuasive smile, taking her look on the chin. "I should have brought them both the same color. It's my fault. You told me that everything had to be equal between them."

"I want red, Mommy," Melissa pleaded.

"Nooooo," Lindsay repeated, though Melissa wasn't bothering her.

Sonny grinned at Angie. "Do you know that she says no the same way that you do? She must hear you stretch it out."

"I don't say *nooooo* that way," Angie responded tersely, not certain why she had to be so ill-humored with him.

Sonny gave Angie's jean covered knee a quick squeeze. "Are you starting fresh for today, or am I still in trouble with you for last night?"

Angie shifted uncomfortably in her seat. "If you bring up anything about last night, or even think about it, I'm not spending the day with you. Do I make myself clear?" she practically hissed at him. She was tired. She hadn't slept well. All night long, her mind kept drawing an image of the two of them kissing.

Sonny flashed Angie a gaze of outrageous pleasantness. She didn't have on any makeup, just a little lipstick. "I'll keep my mouth shut, but take my word for it, you don't want to get inside my head." He liked the fresh-scrubbed look of her face.

"Too much a maze?" Angie rejoined with the beginning of a smile. Even though she fought against it, he had made a dent in her annoyance.

Sonny laughed. "Either that, or an ingrained adolescence."

"Mommy, can I have a red pail?" Melissa asked.

"Yes, if they sell them," Angie sighed. "Uncle Sonny can play with the yellow one."

"Mommy, do you want a pail, too?" Melissa questioned magnanimously, now that she was getting her way.

"No." Angie sent Sonny a bantering grin. "I've made it all the way through my adolescence."

Sonny slid Angie a silent, but visually ribbing touché.

Angie returned the joking confrontation by daring him, with her eyes, to elaborate. The challenge netted her another of his lazy smiles. Then, he started a dialogue with Melissa about the swimming strokes he was going to teach her. Angie joined in, trying hard to keep a lid on her concerns. She'd accepted that she had a tendency to be overly sheltering.

The franchise was located in a shopping strip in a building that had once been occupied by a large food store. The directory at the entrance to the center still read Shopper's Mart. Sonny pulled into a parking spot and they got out of the car. He worked Lindsay out of her seat. She was a handful and needed a firm grip. Meanwhile, Angie assisted Melissa. This was a routine she'd established with Sonny.

Most of the stores were standard fare—a bagel shop, pizzeria, deli, a cleaner, and a drugstore. The drugstore, taking advantage of its new neighbor, had an eye-attracting display of children's swimming tubes, life jackets, and pails and shovels attached to fishnet hanging in one window. Of course, Sonny ran in and bought another red pail, adding life jackets for the girls to his purchase. He'd already thought to get inner tubes, though he hadn't blown them up yet.

He handed Melissa the red pail, and smiled at Angie as she observed the life jackets over his arm.

Angie nodded her approval, and they walked, family-style into "Swimming Babies." Angie carried a tote containing basic necessities—diapers, towels, her bathing suit, underwear for Melissa, the tubes Sonny had brought over along with his dark green boxer-style swimming trunks. She'd allowed the girls to wear their bathing suits under their clothes.

Melissa carried two pails. Lindsay was still hanging on to her original red one for dear life.

It felt like the middle of July inside, a strong contrast to the November chill outdoors. Though they couldn't see the pool from the entry, they could smell it. The air was pungent with the aroma of chlorine.

Sonny had his wallet out before Angie even began to fumble for hers. "Don't even say it," he warned her and then paid for their day's pass.

"Next time," Angie said, her demeanor determined.

Sonny smiled, but didn't actually agree.

There were pegs on two of the putty-colored walls in the lobby. Three-quarters of one wall was already taken up with outerwear. Sonny unzipped his brown leather bomber jacket and slung it over a peg. Then, he maneuvered Lindsay out of her snow jacket. Melissa managed her snow jacket all by herself. Angie hung it up next to her navy pea jacket. A vertical arrow indicated the direction to take for the combination dressing rooms and lavatories.

"Give me my suit and the tubes," Sonny said before they parted.

Angie opened the tote and handed the items over. The exchange left her with a residual sense of intimacy that wasn't unpleasant. Still, she made an effort to ignore the feeling.

"I'll meet you by the pool," Sonny smiled, turning away toward the door lettered with an *M*.

When Angie finally arrived at the pool, Sonny had already staked out four lounges. Angie put her tote down. There were quite a number of families enjoying the large pool. Their chairs were claimed by towels.

Sonny was in his bathing trunks and had blown up the inner tubes. Melissa and Lindsay were wearing matching two-piece pink bathing suits. Lindsay's bulged around her bottom—Angie had left a diaper on underneath.

Sonny's eyes were on Angie. Her legs were bare, but she was still covered from her thighs up with an oversized flannel shirt in a muted blue-and-wine plaid.

"Put my wallet in the bag," he said, holding it out to her. He watched her stick it all the way down for safekeeping. "Are you planning to swim in that shirt?'' he asked, running his index finger across his lower lip.

"I'm not ready to swim yet." She was having trouble with the idea of exposing herself to his gaze. She wouldn't have admitted it, but she didn't want him to find her lacking. Unlike her, he had a perfect physique.

Lindsay started pulling at her diaper. "Off!"

Angie directed her attention to her youngest, glad to get out from under Sonny's concentration. "Will you tell Mommy if you have to go potty?"

Lindsay nodded up and down like a Kewpie doll.

Sonny put the larger of the two life jackets on Melissa, along with a tube. Angie slipped Lindsay's disposable diaper off without having to lower the bottom half of her suit. She handed her over to Sonny, who fastened her into the smaller jacket, then slipped on the other tube.

"Can we go in right now?" Melissa asked, bubbling over.

Sonny hoisted Lindsay up to his shoulder, and took Melissa's hand. "Right now," he said. "If your mother wants to be a killjoy, she can sit here and watch."

Angie watched Sonny edge the girls down into the pool at its lowest end. It only went as deep as three feet. She wanted to be in the water with them having fun. She made a face and used one hand to raise her hair off the back of her neck. It was as hot as a steam bath in here, and Sonny's nudity, though it was perfectly reasonable nudity, ticked her off.

"Hand me a pail?" Sonny called to Angie from the pool. He was just below her feet. He had one hand on the tube around Lindsay. Melissa bobbed at his other side.

Leaning forward, Angie passed him the yellow pail. Before she'd thought to sit back into her terry-padded lounge chair, Sonny had partially filled the pail and thrown the water up at her, soaking the front of her shirt.

Angie shrieked. "You . . . you . . . you're asking for it!"

Sonny's mouth traced a lazy grin. "You're not going to be able to get back at me from up there. Take your shirt off and get in here."

Angie shot Sonny a look that was infused with the full brunt of her exasperation. Then she stood up and started struggling to undo the buttons of her wet shirt.

Sonny watched Angie. "Do you want me to come out with the girls and help you?"

"*Nooooo.*" Angie couldn't keep back a small smile.

Sonny suspected, even before Angie revealed it, that she was wearing a one-piece suit. It was a jungle print and cut modestly. She filled it out just right. She had a great shape.

Angie draped her wet shirt on the back of her chair and got into the pool, feetfirst, right in front of Sonny. Sonny gave a low, throaty growl. Pleased, Angie flushed—but since being obstinate was part of her personality, she gave him a chilly stare.

"Tell the truth . . ." Sonny's suggestive gaze added heat to her flush. "Were you more concerned that I would, or wouldn't?"

Angie tossed him a dumb look. "I don't know what you're talking about."

"You do, but I'll spell it out for you if you'd like." Sonny's tone could have melted winter ice in Alaska.

"No, thank you," Angie retorted.

Sonny said, "I think we're going to have to learn to compromise, before we wear ourselves out."

"Worry about yourself," Angie quipped. "I can hold up my end."

"Mommy," Melissa said. "I want to go on rides."

"Rye . . . rye," Lindsay mimicked.

Angie and Sonny gave each other a smile, and with the girls between them, walked to the levered end of the pool.

Sonny caught Angie fighting back a yawn when they were back at their lounge chairs.

"Sack out for a while," he said affably. "I'll take care of the girls."

Angie slanted him a gaze. "It's pretty sneaky of you, being nice when I'm mad at you."

"Is it working?" Sonny's mouth quirked.

"Not yet," Angie countered.

Sonny grinned. "Lie down, close your eyes and give it a chance."

Angie compromised. She didn't want to miss any of the fun with the girls, but she was exhausted. "I'll just rest for a couple of minutes." Angie glanced at her waterproof watch. It was ten to ten. She settled back on the lounge, and fell asleep as soon as she closed her eyes.

Sonny contemplated Angie in her bathing suit, but he didn't get the time to clear his muddled thoughts. Melissa and Lindsay were frustrating themselves trying to get out of their life jackets.

Angie looked around for Sonny and the girls as soon as she opened her eyes. He was horsing around with them in a huge sandbox, along with other parents and their children. Angie glanced at her watch as she sat up. It was one-fifteen, and her stomach was talking to her.

Angie wrapped a towel around her waist, sarong-style, and went over to the sandbox.

"Did you have a good rest?" Sonny asked.

"Yes." Angie replied. "I'm starved. Aren't you all hungry?"

"We ate." Sonny got to his feet. "What would you like? I'll go get it. They have hamburgers, hot dogs, sandwiches, soup..."

"What did you and the girls have?" Angie asked.

"I had a couple of hamburgers. Melissa polished off a peanut-butter-and-jelly sandwich, a malted, and a banana. Lindsay ate half a peanut-butter-and-jelly sandwich, part of a banana, and some milk."

Melissa rocked on her toes. "Mommy, I ate the crust, too. Uncle Sonny said that we can have ice cream, maybe, when you wake up."

"I-cree," Lindsay said, holding sand in her little pudgy hands.

Angie pretended to give it some thought.

"Come on." Sonny smiled at the girls. "We'll run under the shower while your mother's deciding."

A half hour later, Lindsay and Melissa had a scoop each of soft vanilla ice cream in a cup. Angie had a hamburger and a soda. Sonny went for a dunk in the pool.

Angie was trying to comb her hair into some semblance of order when Sonny came out of the water. He studied the distress on her face while he dried himself off with a towel. "Your hair looks fine, you know."

Angie puckered her lips. "I hate when I can't get my bangs to lay straight over my eyebrows."

Sonny's smile was modified by a look of confusion. "I can't imagine why you want to cover your eyebrows. I know my opinion probably doesn't count, but I like how you look with your eyebrows showing."

Angie slid him a glance, the comb unoccupied in her hand. She would have been flip if she'd had a rejoinder, but she didn't have one. "Thank you, Sonny."

He winked at her. "I wish you'd clued me in sooner that flattery was going to make you nice to me."

Angie laughed. "I'm not thanking you for the flattery."

"What are you thanking me for?" He sat down on the chaise next to her.

"I'm thanking you for today." It had been a long time since she'd felt this content.

"It's been a good day for me, too." He turned his head, trying to cancel his sudden absorption with her face and the look in her sassy chestnut eyes. "The girls fell asleep," he observed.

"Why don't you crash out for a while, too," Angie suggested, knowing he was going to be starting a four a.m.-to-midnight shift.

"Are you sure you don't mind?"

Angie shook her head sincerely.

Sonny and the girls slept. After a while, Angie walked over to the concession stand and bought herself a magazine. She browsed through a number of articles before getting hooked on an installment of a detective story.

"What are you reading?" Sonny asked, startling her.

Angie put the magazine down on her lap. "'Just A Deadbeat.'"

"I read it," Sonny said. "Too bad reality isn't as exciting as fiction."

"Is that why you're in police work? For excitement?"

"No." Sonny sat up. "But it beats being bored." A careless smile deepened the cleft in his chin.

"It's dangerous, Sonny." Angie attacked her lip with her teeth. "Don't you think about that?"

"I don't think any of us think of the risk. We think about the highs. I couldn't begin to describe how I feel when I've collared a drug pusher and gotten him off the street. It's important work, and someone has to do it. I'm good at it, Angie . . . Rick was good at it, too."

Angie lowered her head. It was more than Rick. She was frightened for Sonny. Until that moment, she hadn't realized just how attached she was becoming to him. "Is it a macho thing with you?"

Sonny reached out and slung his arm around her shoulders pulling her close. "No, but a little extra testosterone doesn't hurt."

"Why do you always joke when I'm trying to have a serious conversation with you? Is that your standard operating procedure?"

Sonny gave himself a second to come up with an answer. "I haven't thought about it, but it does seem to me that I'm more glib around you than I am around anyone else."

"Why is that?"

He looked into her studied gaze until she dropped her head and her hair fell over her eyes. "I don't know," he answered truthfully.

"I don't want you to be a cop," Angie whispered against his chest, then pulled away.

"What would you like me to be?" He smiled, trying to offset the waver of tension in her voice. "How about a shoe salesman?"

"There's nothing wrong with selling shoes," Angie responded, her tone strengthening.

"True—not if I were selling women's shoes, and all my customers had legs like yours."

Angie met his eyes squarely. "Are you flirting with me?"

Her blunt question threw him for a second. "Yes," he answered after a pause.

Angie studied him with her head tilted. "To get me to cheer up?"

"Maybe." He had the same feeling he often experienced on an investigation—right before the bottom fell out and all hell broke loose.

"You can't say maybe. That's not an answer." Angie kept her gaze locked on his. "Do you flirt with all women? Is that your style?"

Melissa woke just then. "Mommy, I have to go to the bathroom."

Sonny drew a breath of relief at the reprieve.

"Let's go," Angie said, getting to her feet.

Sonny sat back into his lounge chair and replayed the conversation they'd just had. He couldn't come up with any better responses than the ones he'd given her.

"Mommeee . . ." Lindsay had awoken.

"Hi, Squirt," Sonny smiled. "Mommy will be right back."

"Un-knee . . ." Lindsay sat up and rubbed her eyes. "Pot . . ."

"What?" He was trying to figure out what she was saying.

"Pot," Lindsay repeated. Scampering to her feet, she held her belly.

"Oh, pot." Sonny gulped, fully cognizant. He hiked her up to his shoulder. There was the ladies' room, or the men's room . . . No, he couldn't take her into the men's room . . .

He did a marathon run to the rest rooms praying that Angie would be on her way out when he got there. "Hold it in, Squirt. Okay? For Uncle Sonny . . ."

Angie was stepping out of the ladies' room with Melissa just as Sonny came racing up.

"Switch," Sonny said hoarsely, holding Lindsay out for Angie to grasp. "She said potty."

"You told Uncle Sonny potty?" Angie exalted with Lindsay in her arms. "You are such a good girl...and a big girl."

"How about you compliment her after she's done her business?" Sonny interjected nervously.

Angie sent Sonny a grin and took Lindsay inside.

"Can we go on rides again?" Melissa asked.

"If Mommy says so." Sonny leaned back against the outside wall of the rest room and took some deep calming breaths.

"Uncle Sonny?"

"Yes, Moonbeam."

Melissa tipped her head back to look up. "Why don't I have a daddy?"

"You have a daddy, Moonbeam." Sonny's heart split. "You have an Uncle Sonny Daddy, an Uncle Frankie Daddy, an Uncle Teddy Daddy, and you have a daddy in Heaven."

"Oh..." Melissa was quiet for a second. "I have a lot of daddies."

"And all your daddies love you very much, Moonbeam," Sonny said softly.

"Okay." Melissa smiled, satisfied.

"I want to go on the horse one more time, Mommy," Melissa beseeched. "Just one more."

"Me..." Lindsay poked herself, waving side to side.

They'd been on the carousel a total of six times—twice earlier, and now four times with both Angie and Sonny after swimming. They'd had pizza for dinner, and changed out of their bathing suits. Angie's shirt hadn't dried. She was wearing Sonny's black sweat-shirt, sleeves rolled. He had his undershirt on.

"We'll come back another time." Angie put her foot down. It was clear to her that the girls had had enough for one day.

Sonny lifted Lindsay up. She pressed her face to his neck, seconds away from conking out. "Moonbeam, I promise I'll bring you here again." Sonny used his eyes to punctuate his guarantee to Melissa. "Maybe next time, we'll leave your mother home. She's a party pooper."

By way of retort, Angie regarded Sonny with a long glance that teasingly communicated that she'd like to carve him up like a roast.

The look he gave her back he intentionally orchestrated to be sexy. He did like flirting with her.

Not given a choice, Melissa walked between the adults.

"I don't think they've ever fallen asleep this quickly," Angie said, pretty much tuckered out herself as she relaxed next to Sonny on the couch in her living room.

Sonny raised his head from the back cushion and looked over at her. He wanted to kiss her. He knew he was *going* to kiss her. He didn't care, at the moment, that it was sure to lead to a complicated discussion.

He tangled his fingers into her hair, secured her head and quickly dropped his mouth down to hers. A sigh rushed out between Angie's lips as Sonny caught her by surprise. He used the tip of his tongue to tan-talize her closed teeth. Her lack of involvement didn't restrain him. He knew she was stunned. He also knew what it was like to have her mouth come alive with his . . . and he knew how to get her there.

He kissed her more deeply. Angie's mouth opened without her even being aware. She was dizzy. Sonny dipped his tongue inside, then withdrew, repeating the motion again and again. He could feel her breathing becoming rushed and aroused. Angie clutched his arms with her hands.

"Sonny," Angie whispered on a moan as he swept her bangs from her forehead to kiss her eyebrows one at a time.

"I do like your eyebrows," he said, all husky.

His hand went to her breast as his mouth returned to her lips. Her nipple responded to the first stroke of his thumb. She was firm and perfect, and he wanted to put his mouth there, even if only against his sweatshirt.

"No!" Angie yelled on a quick breath just as Sonny dipped his head to reach his goal. She pushed at him and moved away, stumbling on the coffee table behind her.

Sonny reached out for her, but she quickly caught her balance and stood at a safe distance from him.

"I said no." Her voice was half an order, half a plea. "Don't you understand? No."

Sonny raised his hands in a sign of surrender. "Okay, okay. Did you hurt yourself?"

Angie shook her head and crossed her arms in front of her breasts. "We have to talk. We really have to talk."

Sonny regarded her agitated expression and the swell to her lips that he'd caused. Her hair was in wavy disarray. He didn't want to talk, and he didn't want to do any soul-searching.

"Don't you have anything to say for yourself?"

"Do you want me to apologize?" He was jingling the car keys in his pocket.

"I want us to have a frank discussion about all this."

A grin crossed Sonny's mouth. "Well, frankly Scarlet—"

She cut him off. "This is not the time for you to be a comedian. We have to talk this out. We have to understand where we are both coming from. Where are you coming from, Sonny?"

He "Mirandized" himself. "'You have the right to be silent. Anything you say can be used against you.' You want me to be frank? I'll be frank. I'm attracted to you. Is that frank enough?"

"You cannot be attracted to me. Not really. You just think you are."

Sonny rubbed his thighs with his knuckles. "I really am and I think you're attracted to me, too. Instead of discussing it, why don't we just go with the feeling?"

Angie's expression was intent. "I am not attracted to you, and if I was attracted to you, I still wouldn't go with it."

"Why not?" He rushed right in after her.

Angie fought for composure. "You already know why not. You're too young for me. You're my brother-in-law, and you're a cop."

"That's neat and pat." He understood why she didn't want there to be any chemistry between them. Only, chemistry wasn't something you got to choose. Either it happened, or it didn't happen.

Angie bristled. "Let's just drop it."

But now that it was out there, Sonny didn't want to drop it. "To begin with, I'm not too young for you. I'm older than you in ways you can't measure. There are times that I age ten years in a single day."

That worrisome thought ran around in Angie's head. For now, she didn't let herself chase after it. "I understand why you think you're attracted to me."

"Is that so?" He had no doubt that she was going to lay it out for him. He couldn't wait to hear it.

She'd just figured it out... "You feel an obligation to me and the girls. You're trying to step into your brother's shoes because of it."

Sonny digested and dissected that possibility. "I don't think so," he answered after a pause.

"Maybe you don't realize it on a conscious level." Angie persisted.

Sonny stood up abruptly, startling her with his sudden movement. She swayed.

Sonny put a steadying hand at her waist. "Are you attracted to me because I remind you of Rick?"

Angie rapidly stepped out from his touch. "You don't remind me of Rick at all. I'm too tired to cope with this anymore tonight."

Sonny wasn't going to push her when she wasn't up to being pushed. He had as much thinking to do as she did. He wasn't completely convinced that he wasn't replacing Rick in her eyes. She just might not be aware of it.

"Good night, Angie." He held her eyes for a moment.

"Good night." She let him see himself out, hugging herself within the folds of his shirt that she was wearing. She could smell his scent, and it made her feel pleasantly restless.

Chapter Seven

"Angie, taste the sauce," Connie Falco said. "See what you think."

Angie smiled. "Mom, your sauce is always perfect."

"Taste it anyway." Connie was slicing provolone cheese for the antipasto salad. She was a small woman, narrow through the shoulders. Her gray hair was cut short around her vivacious, slightly lined face. She wore her housedress with knee-high nylons and soft leather oxfords. "Last week, your Aunt Fay commented that I was getting a heavy hand with the garlic."

Angie stuck a spoon into the pot, blew and tasted. "It's perfect, but I don't know why you need to make sauce on Thanksgiving. The turkey is large enough to feed an army."

"And later?" Connie asked impatiently. "If someone wants dinner, am I going to serve turkey again?"

"Of course not." Angie said.

Yawning, Lisa came into the kitchen. "Hi, Angie. Oh, I like your hair that way."

"Thanks." She'd been training it to one side for two weeks now.

"Is that skirt new?"

Angie nodded. "Yes. Do you think this top goes with it?" She'd matched a ribbed turtleneck in a moss green to a flared navy wool skirt—the same navy as her flat-heeled leather boots.

"It goes." Lisa shrugged sleepily. "It just doesn't say anything."

Angie smiled. "Good. I don't feel it's necessary for my clothes to talk."

Lisa shrugged. "Well, at least, you're looking *somewhat* stylish."

Connie asked Lisa, "What time did you get home last night?"

Lisa yawned again. "Ma, don't start. It's Thanksgiving. I'm entitled to go out on a weeknight before a holiday. Is there any coffee left?"

"Entitled..." Connie repeated, with an exaggerated expression that brought dimples to her cheeks. "I've got the pot set up for later, but there's a cupful from this morning in the teapot. Put a light under it."

Lisa walked over to her mother and gave her a hug from the rear. "Isn't she cute when she gets all aggravated with me?"

Connie fought a smile. "Go make yourself the coffee and leave me be. I'm busy."

Lisa turned the jet on under the teapot. "Is anybody else here?"

"Just about everyone," Connie answered, placing hot peppers on the platter she was arranging. "Nancy and Quinn are setting the table downstairs with Aunt Fay. Teddy and Shep are keeping the kids entertained, and by now your father and your Uncle Charlie are down each other's throats about who knows better how to carve the turkey. They started arguing as soon as your father helped me bring the turkey down to cool."

Lisa poured her coffee from the teapot. "Ma, why don't we have holiday dinners in the dining room?"

"It's not large enough." Connie added olives to the platter. "What's wrong with my basement? Do you know how much it cost to have it finished?"

Lisa dropped the subject, looking out the window. "Frankie is here," She observed. "Is anyone else coming?"

"Just Sonny," Connie responded.

"Sonny?" Angie's eyes widened. "You mean Uncle Sonny?"

Connie shook her head. "Aunt Fran and Uncle Sonny went to New Hampshire. I'm talking about *your* Sonny."

Angie swallowed. "Why did you invite him?"

Frankie came in and greeted everyone, then asked, "Ma, do you need me to do anything for you?"

"No, go downstairs," Connie answered.

He took off for the basement immediately.

"I ran into Sonny at the club I was at Saturday night," Lisa remarked, taking a sip of her coffee.

Angie switched her attention from her mother to her sister. "Really..." She hadn't seen or spoken to him since they'd been to "Swimming Babies" more than two weeks ago. "Was he alone?"

"No," Lisa answered. She peered into the refrigerator, obviously looking for something to go with her coffee. "He was with a group."

"All guys?" Angie tried to keep her voice from sounding all that interested.

"Ma, can I have a piece of the cheesecake?" Lisa asked.

"No. That's for later. Make yourself a slice of toast. We're going to eat soon."

"Was the group all guys?" Angie asked a second time, her tone up a pitch.

"What group?" Lisa took out a loaf of white bread and the butter dish.

"The group Sonny was with. Was it all guys?" Angie stuck her hands into the pockets of her skirt.

"No, but I didn't get the feeling they were all paired off. Sonny did dance a few times with one of the women." Lisa popped a slice of bread in the toaster.

"What was she like?" Angie could feel her impatience rising. She thought of pulling Lisa's dark ponytail to get her to be more responsive.

Lisa wiggled her shoulders. "Brunette...built..." Lisa gestured, holding one hand a foot away from her chest. "I don't know why men have such a fixation on breasts."

Angie pulled on the sides of her sweater, looking to stretch it out a bit. It was loose to begin with, but not loose enough to disguise her lack of endowment. "Ma,

I don't know why you had to invite Sonny. You didn't tell him that he could bring anyone with him, did you?''

''He's coming up the walk right now,'' Lisa noted looking out the window.

''Is he alone?'' Angie asked nervously.

Lisa checked. ''Yes. He's holding a couple of bottles of Chianti and a six-pack.''

''Angie, go let him in.'' Connie motioned with her head.

Angie stood rooted to the spot.

''Frankie opened the door downstairs for him,'' Lisa reported, looking over at Angie. ''What's the matter with you? You look kind of pale, and your voice hasn't been sounding right.''

''I'm fine. I got up with a tickle in my throat this morning,'' Angie said, trying to cover up her agitation.

''Are you coming down with something?'' Connie was quick to study Angie with a mother's eagle eye.

''No, Ma.'' Angie shook her head. Certainly nothing that could be cured with medication.

''Angie, here, take the antipasto downstairs.'' Connie held the platter out. ''Lisa, take your coffee and toast and go with Angie. If your Aunt Fay starts up the stairs, tell her I'm coming right down. I don't want her in my kitchen.''

''Ma, you take the antipasto downstairs.'' Angie refused the platter. ''I'll finish for you up here. What else do you have to do?'' At some point, Angie knew, she was going to have to face Sonny, but she wasn't ready yet.

"I have to roll the meatballs and put them in the sauce."

"I'll do it," Angie said swiftly.

"They have to be plump, but not too plump."

Angie went over to the refrigerator for the ground beef that was already seasoned in a bowl. "I'll make the first one for you to inspect—then you won't have to worry."

"All right. Let me see."

Angie washed her hands in the sink, then dug in for a lump of meat and rolled it between her palms. "Okay?" She showed her mother the ball.

"A little plumper. Your Aunt Fay will think I'm being stingy with the meat."

Angie added a little more meat to her hand and rolled again. "How's this?"

Connie tilted her head from side to side. "Put them on a plate first. Make sure they're all the same size before you drop them in the sauce. Lisa, help your sister."

Lisa scowled. "Ma, you know I don't like touching raw meat. I don't even like seeing it."

Connie sent her youngest daughter an exasperated glance. "I hope for your sake that you marry someone who can afford to hire a cook for you."

"I'm planning to, Ma," Lisa countered with a sassy grin.

Connie took the antipasto and headed downstairs.

A few minutes later, Nancy came up to the kitchen, followed by Teddy's wife, Quinn.

"Ma sent us up to help." As usual, Nancy was all dressed up. She were a dusty-blue jersey knit shirt-dress cinched at her waist with a braided leather belt.

"I've got it under control," Angie answered, putting a hand in the bowl.

Quinn, a slim blonde with hazel eyes, was chic even in baggy corduroy slacks and a bulky sweater. She went to the sink and washed her hands. "Let me do some. I need the practice."

Tossing her dark hair, Nancy sat down at the kitchen table across from Lisa. "No matter how well you learn to cook, no Italian male ever thinks his wife cooks as well as his mother."

Quinn smiled. "In my case, Teddy definitely has a point. My best sauce comes straight from the jar."

Lisa shrugged. "I don't think Teddy married you for your cooking."

Quinn grinned and took some meat in her hand. "He certainly knew what he was in for when he married me... but I am trying."

Nancy smiled. "I don't think Teddy would care if he had to have his stomach pumped once a week, as long as he's with you."

Angie joined the laughter, but she wasn't really in the mood. She was too tense about seeing Sonny.

"Ma," Nancy called downstairs when the meatballs were all in the pot. "Do you want us to bring everything else down now?"

"Yes," Connie returned. "The extra stuffing, yams, vegetables and artichokes are in the oven. Put everything on trays. Use mitts. There's cranberry sauce in a bowl in the refrigerator."

Angie carried the tray with the stuffing. She was last in line as they marched down the stairs. *Please,* she prayed silently, *don't let me trip and fall in front of Sonny.*

"Hi, Angie." Sonny nodded at her. He was holding a ball.

"Sonny." Angie nodded back with barely a glance.

Sonny followed her with his eyes. Angie continued walking toward the picnic tables that had been brought in from outdoors and covered with plastic cloths.

"Uncle Sonny, throw the ball," Melissa squealed.

Sonny forced his eyes off Angie's retreating form, and threw Melissa the ball. He'd purposely stayed away from her, wanting to give them both a chance to recover.

"Everyone to the table," Connie announced, seated on a bench with Fay and Charlie.

Angie tried to avoid sitting next to Sonny, but she wound up at his side. Angie edged closer to Lindsay, who sat in a booster chair to her left. Taking his cue from her action, Sonny edged nearer to Melissa, who was on his right.

Angie put some cranberry sauce on Lindsay's plastic plate. Holding the bowl, she leaned forward to look over at Melissa.

"Would you like me to put some of that on her plate?" Sonny asked.

"Yes, please." Her politeness was as pronounced as his.

"Too much, Uncle Sonny," Melissa protested as he dumped it on.

Sonny took some off her plate and put it on his. He passed the bowl across to Quinn, who put just a spoonful in front of her son, T.J. The one-year-old immediately pounded it to mush on his high-chair tray.

"You still protecting the Bronx?" Anthony Falco asked Sonny.

"Doing my best."

Angie caught a glimpse of Sonny's congenial smile from the corner of her eye. She was intent on keeping him out of her direct visual field.

"A house was broken into just two blocks from here last week. The owners were away on vacation." Anthony conversed with a watchful eye on the platter of antipasto as it made the rounds of the table. From his thin build, one would never have guessed just how much food he could pack away.

"It was fortunate that they weren't home." Sonny accepted a can of beer from Frankie.

Connie sighed. "Brooklyn isn't what it used to be."

"I keep telling you to move out to Long Island," Fay inserted, repeating a familiar refrain. She was Connie's youngest sister. There was a family resemblance, but Fay was shorter and heavier-set.

"What?" Connie retorted dismissively. "They don't have any thieves on Long Island?"

"They do, but they mostly commute into the city to work." Fay's pudgy husband, Charlie contributed the one-liner. He owned a pizzeria on Long Island, but he would have much preferred being a stand-up comic. He was fond of saying that he would have followed his dream if he'd had the face for it. No one had ever asked him exactly what kind of face he thought he needed to have.

"Do thieves come where we live?" Kim, one of Nancy and Shep's twin daughters, asked.

"They don't come where we live," Shep answered in a reassuring tone. He made a V of his fingers to push the wire frames on his glasses closer to his brown eyes. He projected a more studious appearance than the other young men at the table, but he was no less nice-looking.

"They can, if they want to." Stephie, the other seven-year-old twin, supplied.

Belatedly, Anthony realized he shouldn't have brought the topic up. "Who's going to have some wine?"

Quinn lifted her hand. Teddy took the bottle from his father. He poured some out for his wife. Before Quinn had a chance to take a taste, Teddy nosedived in to place a quick kiss across her lips.

"Don't you ever stop?" Lisa scowled comically.

"I've been away for a whole week," Teddy countered while Quinn smiled and sent her husband a private message with her eyes.

"Would you like some wine?" Sonny asked Angie without fully looking her way. Teddy and the bottle were an arm's reach from him.

"Yes, thank you," Angie said in a modulated tone without turning her head.

Sonny poured for her. Angie reached for the glass before he'd quite stopped. Some wine spilled on the table. Angie and Sonny both pulled their white paper napkins out from under their silverware to mop up.

Their knuckles touched. Angie immediately withdrew her hand.

Sonny's eyes flew to Angie's face, but she dodged his regard. "It was my fault. I've got it," he apologized.

"I'll get more napkins and a sponge." Though she tried not to, Angie had to press her back to Sonny's side while she bent her knee and swung her leg to extricate herself from the bench.

As soon as Angie was out of earshot, Nancy asked, "Is she okay?" She aimed the question at Sonny. Everyone in the family knew how much time they'd been spending together—how close they'd become. It was natural to look to him for an assessment.

Uncomfortable, Sonny shrugged. "I think she's okay." But if her emotions were anything like his, then she was far from okay. She was making it clear that she didn't want him to be here. He'd come because he'd wanted to see her. He couldn't keep himself from wanting to see her. He'd hoped they could get back to where they'd been before they'd had the discussion that hadn't got either of them anywhere.

There was continuous chatter throughout the meal, though Angie was conspicuously quiet. Sonny managed to be outwardly social, contradicting his inner stress. Two and a half hours later, the women cleared the table of what was left of the food. The kids begged to watch cartoon videos that their grandparents kept for them in the den. Teddy and Shep herded them upstairs, settled them in front of the TV and put the twins in charge.

Anthony and Charlie decided to take a walk, and they went up for their coats.

Soon, Angie, Nancy, Quinn and Lisa came down from the kitchen. Connie and Fay had taken over upstairs.

"Since I promised not to watch football today," Teddy said, addressing the guys, "how about some poker?" Pitching Quinn a tongue-in-cheek look, he added, "Is that okay with you, hon?"

Quinn nodded and smiled.

"I think there's something wrong between Angie and Sonny," Nancy whispered to Lisa as they stood apart from the others.

Lisa agreed with a nod. "Angie, Quinn," Lisa beckoned to the two of them. "Come up to my room. I want to show you the new dress I just bought."

Seated at the picnic table with Teddy, Frankie and Shep, Sonny watched Angie go back upstairs. Heavy-hearted, he flicked the tab off another can of beer.

"What's going on between you and Sonny?" Lisa asked, hanging her new dress back up.

"I don't know what you mean." Angie sat stiffly between Nancy and Quinn on Lisa's bed.

"Did you and Angie have a fight?" Teddy asked, laying down two cards.

"Not exactly." Sonny stared at a pair of jacks and a pair of fives in his hand. He wasn't feeling any excitement knowing he had a practically surefire shot at winning.

* * *

"There's just been some weirdness between us," Angie finally admitted when the prodding didn't let up.

"What do you mean, weirdness?" Nancy questioned.

Angie's tension showed. She crossed her legs, but couldn't quite sit still. She kicked one leg back and forth. "He thinks he's attracted to me."

"We've been getting close," Sonny explained. "We've been laughing and kidding around. I like being with her. I really like being with her. She's been comfortable with me...but now she's not. I guess you've noticed..."

"What made her stop feeling comfortable?" Frankie asked, folding his cards on the deal.

"I suppose I got too physical with her." Sonny picked up a third five for the odd card he'd discarded. The phrase, *lucky in cards, unlucky in love,* played in his head. He threw his full house facedown on the table.

"Are you saying that you took advantage of her?" Teddy's voice held an edge.

"I kissed her a few times. That's all," Sonny assured Teddy. "But the physical thing is out there between us. She feels it just like I feel it... Well, I might feel it stronger than she does. Actually, I'm sure I do feel it stronger than she does."

"So, what are you saying?" Teddy asked. "Are you looking to put the make on her?"

Sonny felt his temper climb another rung. "I have nothing but respect for Angie."

"He's my brother-in-law," Angie exclaimed with exasperation.

"That isn't a reason for you not to be attracted to him," Quinn replied.

"It isn't," Nancy seconded. "He's not a blood relation."

"Well, let me tell you something." Angie stood and faced the three women. "I was sixteen when Rick and I started to date. Do you know how old Sonny was then? He was ten!"

Nancy grinned. "He's not a little boy anymore."

"That is not the point," Angie flew off the handle. "When I'm forty, he be thirty-four. When I'm . . ."

"When you're eighty, he'll be seventy-four," Quinn finished off. "So what?"

"So he's a cop," Angie threw in the kicker as she circled back from her walk around the room. "That's what. I will never let myself fall in love with another cop."

"It's hard to fight chemistry," Quinn said.

"I intend to fight it," Angie declared with determination. "As far as chemistry goes, Sonny might very well be mistaking chemistry with a feeling that he wants to do right by his brother's wife and kids."

Sitting on the carpet cross-legged, Lisa commented, "I think guys have a pretty clear idea about chemistry, and I don't believe the notion comes from their heads."

* * *

"She cares about you," Frankie informed Sonny. "You know when I called you last week to shoot the breeze, it was Angie who asked me to call. She was in a panic because she hadn't heard from you. She had you lying in an alley somewhere."

Sonny felt like the worst kind of heel for making her upset, but he also felt a wild thumping of his heart that she'd been so concerned. "I was leaving her alone because I thought that was what she wanted."

Frankie nodded. "I'd say we're lucky if we can figure out fifty percent of the time what they want."

Sonny rubbed his face in his hands. "I just don't know what to do. I want her to be happy. I want to keep her laughing."

"It sounds to me like you're falling in love with her," Shep evaluated.

Sonny ran that premise around in his mind. Not only did it sound that way, it felt that way. It was a surprise to him that the realization didn't come as a shock.

"The subject is closed. I don't want to talk about this anymore. Nothing is going to happen between us," Angie said doggedly.

Lisa made a waving motion with her hand. "I think you and Sonny are right for each other."

Angie flicked Lisa an out-of-joint look. "I'm going to check on the kids."

Nancy, Quinn and Lisa trailed Angie to the door. Angie did not see the knowing looks the three women exchanged.

* * *

"I hope you're winning," Nancy said, coming up behind Shep.

"How can he be?" Lisa sassed. "We all know that Frankie cheats."

Frankie crooked a finger at Lisa. "Come here. I want to whisper something in your ear." The joking gleam in his dark eyes intentionally suggested something else.

Lisa put a thumb to her nose and wagged her fingers.

Quinn got her bottom pinched the moment she stepped next to Teddy. "Stop it, Teddy," she protested, giggling.

Angie came downstairs. Sonny's eyes immediately went to her, then skidded away.

Teddy had his rascal eyes on Quinn. "What were the four of you doing upstairs so long? Gossiping?"

"Oh, and men don't gossip," Quinn countered.

"We do not gossip," Teddy responded, standing up for his side. "We discuss." Teddy, Frankie and Shep eyed Angie, who was hanging back from the group.

Quinn, Nancy and Lisa zeroed in on Sonny. In the same instant, Angie and Sonny realized what the talk on both fronts had been about.

Sonny focused on Angie. Her cheeks were tinted a becoming pink.

"Sonny," Angie said, speaking his name tightly. "Could I see you upstairs for a moment?"

"Uh-oh," the guys teased Sonny in unison.

Sonny winked at them as he got up from the table.

Brewing a storm, Angie led the way upstairs with Sonny right behind her.

Connie called from the living room where she was sitting with Fay, "Angie, plug in the coffeemaker while you're in the kitchen."

"Yes, Ma," Angie returned over her shoulder.

Anthony and Charlie entered the kitchen from the outside door just as Angie stepped in with Sonny. Angie plugged in the coffee machine, then jerked her head toward Sonny, motioning for him to follow her.

She marched to the hall closet and got her pea jacket.

"Is your jacket up here?" she asked, in none too friendly a tone.

Sonny gathered they were going out. "Frankie took it from me when I got here. I guess he hung it up."

Angie stepped aside so that Sonny could have a look.

The brown leather bomber jacket was in the closet. Sonny put it on over his plum-and-hunter-colored rugby shirt.

"Where are the two of you going?" Connie asked as Angie and Sonny walked by the living room.

"We're just getting some air," Angie answered without breaking her stride.

Angie turned and faced Sonny as soon as they were out of the house. At five o'clock it was already dark, but he could see her in the light from the outdoor bulb.

It had started snowing sometime earlier, and flakes were still falling. The ground was turning into a virgin burst of white.

"We should get the kids and bring them out here," Sonny said, smiling.

"You told my brothers and Shep about us," Angie accused angrily, ignoring his suggestion.

"You told your sisters and Quinn," Sonny retorted.

"That's different!"

"How is it different?"

Angie exhaled, visibly fuming in the frosty air. "I want to know exactly what you said."

"What did *you* say?" He was going tit for tat with her, only he wasn't angry.

"I asked you first." Angie kicked snow with her boot, trying to find release for some of her frustration.

"I'll think about telling you if you pull your collar up," Sonny returned.

Her face was bright with the cold, and her hair was covered with snow. The air was hazy all around them, and they were both breathing with their mouths slightly open.

Angie barely suppressed the temptation to slug him. Reaching down, she grabbed a handful of snow and threw it his way.

Sonny wiped his face. "Is that how you want to do this?" His manner was a blend of sexiness and teasing.

"I'm trying to get you to cooperate with me," Angie said through clenched teeth, keeping an eye on his hands.

"Oh, you want cooperation?" Sonny grinned. "Why didn't you say so?"

Angie watched him reach down and scoop up some snow. His hand was large enough for him to grab a healthy amount of it.

"Don't you dare throw it at me," Angie warned, circling around him without turning her back.

Sonny used his free hand to grab her in a hammer-lock that was firm, but not crushing.

"You make me so mad sometimes," Angie said, struggling to pull free, but only partially miffed now. The silliness of this scene was having its effect on her.

Sonny dropped the snow and turned her into his chest, jerking her close. "I didn't say anything you wouldn't want me to say. Besides, Teddy will tell Quinn, and Shep will tell Nancy. It will get back to you. How about if you just tell me what you said?"

Angie smiled, caught herself and grimaced. "I said you were a pain in the neck."

"Was that the best you could do?" Sonny grinned.

"Actually, I did better. I'm just censoring it now."

"That's my girl..." Sonny flicked some snow from her hair. "Let's go to a movie Saturday night. What do you say?"

She took a second. She wanted very much to say yes, which was, of course, the reason she said, "I can't. I've made plans." It was a lie.

Sonny let her go to look into her face. "What plans?"

Angie thought as quickly as she could. "Nancy set up a blind date for me."

"Oh..." That information cut right through him.

"Well...ah..." Angie dropped her gaze to the ground.

The front door opened. Connie stuck her head out. "How do you like that? It's snowing... What are you two doing standing in the snow? Come in the house. We're waiting coffee for you."

"I'm going to have to be going," Sonny responded. "I've got early duty tomorrow. Thanks for having me. Dinner was wonderful. Please say goodnight to everyone for me."

"Good night," Angie said, feeling miserable as he looked at her.

"See you," Sonny replied with a nonchalance he had to work on achieving.

Angie stamped her boots at the front door as Sonny walked to his car.

Chapter Eight

Saturday afternoon found Angie jumpy and restless. The surprisingly early snow had continued from Thanksgiving through Friday. The girls had been cranky confined indoors. She'd entertained them with as much inventiveness as she could dredge up. She'd kept herself busy doing chores around the apartment that she'd put off. This morning they'd gone to the park and played in the snow. That had been good...but it would have been better if Sonny had been with them.

Angie turned the radio on in the kitchen, low enough not to carry out of the room. The girls were taking a nap. She turned in to the most jangling rock she could find on the dial, matching her agitated state of mind.

The kitchen had a country decor. The linoleum was a grid of beige-and-green squares. As always, the almond-colored appliances sparkled. Today, even the wallpaper—a patchwork of paisley prints that had been up for over five years—gleamed like new. Scrubbing the walls was a task she'd taken upon herself when she hadn't been able to relax the evening before in front of the TV.

Angie poured herself a cup of coffee from the pot she'd brewed that morning. A jolt of caffeine was hardly something she needed. She added milk and sugar, turned the radio down, went to the phone and dialed her sister's number.

"Hello," Nancy said on the other end.

"Hi." Angie took a sip. "It's me. What are you doing?"

"Watching Shep try to hang shelves in the living room. What are you doing?"

"Nothing..." Angie took another sip. "Did you ask Shep what I asked you to ask him?"

"About Sonny?" Nancy inquired, all innocence.

"You know perfectly well that's what I mean. You can just get that grin off your face." Angie was more bothered by her own behavior than Nancy's. She felt as if she'd reverted to fourth-grade antics.

Nancy didn't try to hide her laugh. "I asked him. He said that he thinks he's in love with you."

Angie sputtered, swallowing wrong. She had to put her cup down to wipe her chin with a dish towel. "Sonny said that he thinks he's in love with me?"

"No. Shep told Sonny that it sounds as if he's in

love with you after Sonny went on and on about how he wants you to be happy.''

''What did Sonny say after Shep said that?''

''He didn't say anything.''

''Did Shep say how he looked when he wasn't saying anything?''

Nancy grinned. ''He didn't say, but as long as we're talking this out, I do want to make a point. First of all, I don't think that what Sonny is feeling has anything to do with any obligation. I don't get the difference between your falling in love with him secretly, or falling in love with him in the open. Either way, you're still going to worry about his being a cop. Your way, you don't get to have any of the perks. I don't understand your logic.''

Angie dived into her obstinacy. ''I never said I was falling in love with him. And I don't want to have a logical discussion with you right now. If you're not going to agree with me, I'm hanging up.''

''I've got to go anyway,'' Nancy said. ''Shep's calling me.''

Angie hung up after Nancy left her with a dead line. Muttering, she yanked the receiver back off its cradle on the wall.

''You are a grown woman,'' Angie lectured herself while she dialed. ''An adult. Get your act together. You can be friendly without it meaning anything more than that.''

Sonny answered on the fifth ring. He was just walking into his studio apartment. He'd been at the gym, working his muscles until they'd cramped. With his conditioning, it took a lot of hard work to get himself into a knot.

"Hello."

"It's Angie." Turning the mouthpiece to the side, Angie blew out a breath. Her edginess had amplified.

"Hi." Sonny felt his pulse kick right up again, as if he'd just stepped off the handball court.

Angie picked up a decided aloofness in his voice. "I guess you're not on duty this weekend?" Of course, he wasn't on duty... He'd asked her to go to the movies tonight. Why couldn't she have just said yes?

Sonny shrugged out of his jacket. "I'm off this weekend." What did she want from his life? he asked himself.

"So...ah...what are you doing for dinner?" Obviously, he wasn't going to make this easy for her. "I thought you might like to come over. I'm making—" Angie pulled the phone cord as far as it went. It didn't get her quite close enough to the freezer above her refrigerator. She had to balance on her toes and lean forward. She nearly fell before she got a grip on the handle. "Chicken parmigiana," she finished.

"Tonight?" Was she saying that the guy she was going out with wasn't going to spring for a meal? "Where is your date taking you?"

She had every intention of telling him she'd lied about having a date. Only she couldn't do it over the phone. She'd tell him after he stopped being stubborn and came over. "To the movies," she fibbed again.

Cheapskate, Sonny decided.

"Are you coming over for dinner?" Angie made herself sound as detached as he was sounding.

"Sure, what time?" He figured he might just hang around long enough to meet her jerk of the week.

"Six. I'll feed the girls first."

"Fine." Sonny hung up.

Angie slammed her phone down. She didn't have a clue why she was angry, but she was angry.

Sonny knocked on the door precisely at six. He'd brought a bottle of wine over, but on second thought left it in his car. Not too late, he'd realized he'd been about to get her mellow for someone else.

Angie eyeballed him through the peephole long enough to decide that he didn't look any friendlier than he'd sounded on the phone.

She put a strained hostess kind of smile on her face and opened the door.

"Hi," he said. He walked in as she stepped to the side. He wasn't angry with her. Not exactly. He was angry that she'd accepted a blind date at this point— he'd expected her to realize they were beyond all that now. He was angry that he couldn't find his balance.

"Hi," Angie answered uncomfortably, losing her smile. She took his jacket and hung it up. Where was his usual easygoing behavior?

Melissa ran into the hallway. "Uncle Sonny, do you want to see the picture I'm making?"

"I'd love to, Moonbeam." Sonny flashed a smile, and let Melissa lead him off to the living room.

"I'm going to finish up in the kitchen," Angie called after him, without getting any response.

They ate at the dining-room table so that they could keep tabs on the girls. Melissa and Lindsay were in their pajamas. They were watching *Sleeping Beauty* on video. It didn't matter how many times they saw it, they were always enthralled.

"Very good," Sonny said after his first taste of the chicken parmigiana. The chicken was slightly burned under the covering of melted cheese. It didn't matter to him. He wasn't that in tune with his taste buds.

"Thank you," Angie responded stiffly without making eye contact with him, not that she hadn't attempted a glance.

Sonny swirled spaghetti with his fork against a spoon. He tried not to notice the way her hair glistened, and that she'd brushed it off her forehead just the way he liked it. "So, who do you have watching the girls tonight?"

"I'm taking them to Nancy's to spend the night." *When first one practices to deceive...* "You don't have to eat the chicken." She pulled at him with her eyes. "I know I burned it."

He wondered if she knew what she did to his libido when she looked at him like that. "It's not that bad," he replied without inflection, using his knife to saw under the cheese and into the too firm crust.

Angie tasted again for herself. It *was* that bad. "I suppose you have plans for this evening?" she asked after she'd chewed and swallowed.

He thought of telling her he did, but... "I don't have any plans." He knew she was attracted to him. The way she had kissed him, and held on to him, and the low murmurs that had escaped her throat told him that. But sexual attraction was sexual attraction. He knew, too well, that it didn't have to mean more than physical desire. He'd been honing that premise until he'd decided to get close to her.

Now, Angie told herself. *Tell him now that you made up the blind date bit.* She twirled her spaghetti, thinking it over.

"What time is he picking you up?" Sonny force-fed himself more chicken.

"Uh..." She looked at him as if he were speaking a foreign language that she had to translate into English. "We're meeting there." She finally got it out.

"Where?" His instincts and senses were trained to be alert. Her hesitancy hadn't gone by him unnoticed. Only, he didn't know what to make of it. Did she suspect that he'd been thinking of sticking around to meet the guy?

"Where?" Angie repeated.

"Where are you meeting him?"

"At the movies."

"How are you going to know him?"

Angie's bright eyes sparked the distance of the table between them and connected with Sonny's crystal blue gaze. "He's going to be carrying a red rose," she blurted out.

Was this guy a cartoon character, or what? "What movie are you planning to see?"

"We decided we'd decide there." Her language skills, Angie decided, could use an overhaul.

"What time are you supposed to meet?" Sonny raised an eyebrow, and put his fork and spoon down. The spaghetti was fine, but he'd had it with eating.

"Eight o'clock." Make something of that, Angie challenged with her eyes.

Sonny glanced at his watch. "It's a quarter to seven. Shouldn't you be getting ready?" She was wearing jeans and a light blue sweatshirt, sleeves pushed up to her elbows.

"Is it that time already?" Angie feigned anxiety. "You're right. I should be getting changed." Pushing her seat back, Angie got to her feet. She was even more ticked off at him than she'd been earlier. He could have given her the leeway to confess.

Sonny picked his fork back up. "I hope you don't mind if I finish eating before I leave?"

"It's your stomach," Angie countered, walking away.

She sat on her bed after closing her bedroom door and looked at her watch. She figured twenty minutes. It couldn't take him any longer than that to finish his meal—unless he went into the kitchen for seconds. She hadn't ruined the spaghetti by cooking it too long.

Sonny took Angie's dish and silverware into the kitchen. He scraped her plate, rinsed it and set it into the dishwasher. He gave a thought to clearing up the kitchen for her, but he rejected the idea as soon as it came. Why would he want to help her be on time for her date?

He went to the refrigerator and got out a bottle of beer. She'd already served him beer in a glass. He went back to the dining-room table and drank this one straight from the bottle. He didn't know what he had to gain by hanging around.

At a quarter after seven, Angie came out of her bedroom. She skidded to a stop, seeing Sonny still at the table.

"You're still eating?" She'd given him a full half hour. What was his problem?

Sonny quickly stuffed a wedge of cold, burned chicken into his mouth.

Angie had to wait for him to finish chewing before he spoke.

"You haven't changed," he said finally, commenting on the obvious.

Angie thought quick. "I'm having trouble deciding what to wear. And my throat is a little dry. I came out to get some soda." She swung into the kitchen.

"Hell," Sonny cursed under his breath. How much thinking did she have to put into this date?

Angie passed him with a can of soda in her hand. She glanced into the living room at the girls. Lindsay had fallen asleep on the carpet with her teddy bear under her head. Melissa was singing along with the Seven Dwarfs.

Angie went back to her bedroom.

Sonny took his plate into the kitchen. Since he couldn't come up with any other reason to stay, he started cleaning up. He didn't have the slightest idea why he was insisting on sticking his nose in her face.

He wasn't by nature addicted to aggravating himself. . . .

At seven-thirty Angie came into the kitchen. She knew he was there. She'd heard the noise. It had taken her all of ten minutes to throw on a change of clothes.

Sonny scoped her, gaze traveling from turtleneck to skirt to boots with an almost imperceptible flicker. He wasn't going to tell her she looked nice, but he did give her a nod.

"I guess I'll be going," Angie said, fidgety.

"Have a good time," Sonny answered tightly.

Angie couldn't come up with anything else to do, but leave. She went to the hall closet, pulled out her pea jacket and went out the door.

In less than five minutes, Sonny realized that she'd forgotten to take the girls to Nancy's. He first considered driving them over there himself. Only, he knew Lindsay had fallen asleep and it seemed a shame to wake her. There wasn't any reason why he couldn't stay and baby-sit. Actually, he liked the idea of waiting for her to come home.

Sonny went to the phone, got Nancy's number from an information operator and dialed.

"Hello," Nancy answered.

"Hi, Nancy. It's Sonny DeFranco. I just wanted you to know that there's been a change in plans. Angie is not going to bring the girls over. I'm going to watch them."

"I didn't know Angie was planning to bring the girls over," Nancy said, puzzled. "Where is she going?"

That little imp, Sonny thought with a grin. "You didn't set her up on a blind date tonight?"

"No," Nancy responded cautiously. "Is everything all right there?"

"Everything is fine." Sonny felt a ton's worth of frustration lift off his shoulders. "Do me a favor, Nancy? Don't mention to her that I called you. Okay?"

"All right," Nancy agreed.

"Bye, Nancy."

"Bye, Sonny."

Sonny had no sooner hung up the phone when Angie rushed breathlessly into the apartment. Sonny heard the door open and went out to the hall.

"I don't know where my head is," she said. "I'm supposed to take the girls to Nancy's." She'd been taking a walk around the complex of apartments when she remembered that she'd included the girls in her farce.

Sonny attempted to play it straight. He understood her motive for all this. She was running from him— running from the feelings they'd been sharing. "Lindsay is already asleep. It would be a pity to wake her. I'll stay and baby-sit."

Angie felt stupid, stubborn and childish—not that she was going to let any of that stop her. "No. Really..."

"I absolutely insist. Call Nancy and tell her there's been a change in plans."

Angie let out a long breath between her teeth. What was she supposed to do now? And why was he looking at her that way? "What is that look on your face?"

"Indigestion," Sonny suggested, teasing. He couldn't wait to laugh with her when she finally confessed.

"Hmm," Angie returned, gauging him with her head cocked to one side. She had the distinct impression that she was missing a joke.

"You're going to be late. Call Nancy." He took her by the hand and practically dragged her to the phone.

Without any option, Angie lifted the receiver from the wall phone and dialed after shrugging Sonny aside. "Hi, Nancy. Listen, Sonny is going to baby-sit. I won't be bringing the girls over."

"...with a forty percent chance of rain late Sunday," came across the line.

"I know I'm going to have a good time," Angie said on her end, looking Sonny in the face. "Of course, I'll call you tomorrow. Bye."

Sonny guessed, while admiring her spunk, that she'd either dialed for the time or the weather. He knew she hadn't called Nancy. "You'd better step on it."

Angie gave an inadequate gesture with her hand. "Are you sure you don't mind baby-sitting?"

"I'm positive." Sonny said, smiling, waiting for her to come clean.

"Well, I'm going," Angie said, stressed. Where was she supposed to go with two—two and a half hours or so to kill?

This time Sonny walked her out to the hall.

"Your indigestion seems to be getting worse," Angie commented through her teeth when he opened the front door for her. She was having a problem defining that look on his face.

"I'll survive." Sonny grinned. "If you're going, you'd better hurry... Unless, you don't really want to go."

Now or never, Angie said to herself. "Of course, I want to go. Why wouldn't I want to go?" She purposefully walked out.

Sonny closed the door. The way he read it, she had two choices. Come back in and admit what she'd been up to, or waste some time. He put his money on the latter. She was too stubborn for anything else.

Angie considered going over to the mall for her fake date, then decided she needed to walk off some of the tension seeing Sonny had brought on. How did he manage to stir her up so much?

Sonny picked Lindsay up and carried her to bed. Melissa's eyes were still glued to the TV screen. The Prince was about to wake Sleeping Beauty with a kiss.

"It's time for bed." Sonny said, coming back into the living room as the credits were rolling.

"Will you tell me a story, Uncle Sonny?" Melissa asked, too tired to put up a fight.

Sonny agreed, but decided to make up his own instead of reading aloud from one of the girls' books. When he was done, the girls looked sleepy, but pleased with his fairy tale.

"I didn't know there could be a mommy princess." Melissa said sleepily.

"They're definitely around," Sonny answered, sitting at the side of the bed.

"Do they get to have a Prince Charming?"

"They do after they stop being stubborn."

"Why is the mommy princess stubborn?"

"She's stubborn because she's afraid to love the Prince Charming."

Melissa yawned. "Is the Prince Charming going to kiss her?"

Sonny smiled. "He sure is, and he's going to wipe her stubbornness away."

Angie filed in line at the Multiplex three blocks away. Was there anything more humiliating than going to the movies alone on a Saturday night? She couldn't think of anywhere else to go and it would kill time before she headed back home. Home to Sonny.

Her exasperation was gathering momentum as she shuffled along among couples of varying ages. Every single one of the twosomes were getting on her nerves—especially the ones that appeared joined at the hip.

"Angie?"

Angie looked up from her aisle seat into the face of her insurance agent. "Richie..."

"I thought I saw you walk in." Richard Walker smiled. "You're here alone, right?"

Angie bit the bullet and nodded.

"Why don't we find two seats together?"

Sonny checked his watch again. It was almost midnight. Where was she? Had she called Lisa from the outside and gone somewhere with her? Was she with

Frankie? Had Teddy picked her up? Had she gone over to a friend's house?

"That was the best cheesecake ever." Angie smiled at Richie as he walked her to her front door. They'd sat in a diner talking for over an hour without a professional desk between them. He was thirty-nine. He'd been divorced for six years. No children. His hair was dark, his eyes brown, his build more compact than muscular. His features combined to make a nice face. He wasn't strikingly handsome, but there was a sort of quiet sexiness about him.

Richie nodded. "I had a real nice time tonight. Do you think we could do it again?"

"I'd like that," Angie answered.

"Let's make it definite. Are you free for dinner at all during the week?"

"I'd have to see if I can get someone to baby-sit."

"Whatever night is good." Richie's warm smile reached his eyes. "I'll leave it to you."

Angie fit her key into the lock.

Sonny saw the front knob turn. He'd been marching the hallway inside the apartment. He pulled open the door ready to haul her into his arms. Instead, he got the wind knocked out of his sails.

"Who are you?" Sonny asked, shocked, staring at Angie's companion.

Angie made the introductions. "Sonny, this is Richard Walker. Richie, this is my brother-in-law, Sonny DeFranco."

Richie put out his hand. A beat later, Sonny accepted a shake.

Richie directed himself back to Angie. "I'll call. Try hard. Okay?"

"Okay." Angie smiled.

Sonny kicked the door shut after Angie stepped in. "You didn't have any problem with the girls, did you?" she asked, taking her pea jacket off.

"No problem with the girls," Sonny responded tersely.

Angie hung her jacket up and turned to face him. "There's something I feel I should tell you..."

Sonny raised his hand to stave her off. "Let me take a stab. You didn't have a blind date for tonight."

There was dead silence. Angie got flushed. He caught her by surprise knowing what she'd been about to tell him.

Sonny explained before she asked. "I called Nancy the first time you left the apartment. I wanted to let her know that I was going to baby-sit."

"Oh..." Angie was flustered and angry. He could have kept her from making an idiot of herself.

"Where does Walker fit in?" Sonny was steaming.

"I met him at the theater." Angie walked into the living room to sit down. It was much too tense standing with him in the hallway.

Sonny was right behind her. He didn't take a seat. "You let some stranger pick you up? I don't want to think about what could have happened to you." Sonny's voice was low, but as angry as she'd ever heard him.

"It wasn't like that," Angie retorted. What did he take her for? "We know each other. He's my insurance agent. We just happened to meet at the theater.

He was there alone. I was there alone. We saw the movie together, and we went for coffee afterward."

Sonny hunkered down in front of her, getting their faces level. "Why did you do it?" He thought he knew, but maybe he didn't. He was only sure that she made him nuts.

Angie kept her eyes downcast. "I did it because I needed to do it. When I'm with you, I can't think logically. When I'm not with you, I know what's best for me."

Sonny could feel his heart in his throat. "What if I wasn't a cop?"

"You are a cop." Her voice barely made it above a whisper.

"I don't see you and the girls as an obligation." He wanted to be sure of the exact extent of their stalemate.

Angie nodded her head, her eyes on her lap where her hands tightly held her knees. She wasn't going to let herself think of Nancy's reasoning. She did know what was best for her.

Sonny gave in finally to the futility of butting heads with her. He'd kept a cap on his pride long enough. "I still intend to spend time with my nieces."

Angie compressed her lips and swallowed. "I want you to."

Angie didn't look up until she heard the front door close. Then, she wiped the tears streaming down her face with the back of her hands.

Chapter Nine

Angie drove into the parking spot that she paid for along with her rent. As she turned the engine off, she noticed Sonny. He was leaning against the fender of his car in one of the guest spaces. He was fighting the wind in a topcoat with his collar up around his neck. There was less than an hour left of winter daylight. The cold was becoming more intense as the temperature dropped with the graying of sunset.

Angie had seen him now and again in the last couple of weeks, but never unexpectedly. He always called first to make arrangements to spend time with the girls. He took them out individually or together, never asking her to join in. Her heart sank every single time, even if it was for the best.

Her hair whipping toward her face, Angie walked over to him. "I took the girls to my mother's this morning. They're staying there tonight.'' She was amazed at the way she'd mantained an even tone with her heart doing cartwheels. She was better prepared for his presence when it was planned—not that she was ever immune. She did a lot of wondering about how long it was going to take her to become immune.

"Lindsay left her teddy bear in the back of my car. I noticed it when I got to work this morning. I know how attached she is to that bear. I thought I should get it back to her as quickly as I could.'' Sonny crammed his hands into the pockets of his coat, feeling intrusive and tense.

"I turned her room upside down this morning, looking for it.'' Angie shivered, not from the weather. She couldn't tear her eyes from his face. "Have you been waiting long?''

"Just a few minutes. I saw your car coming down the street.'' Get the bear. Give it to her and leave, he commanded himself. His adrenaline was pumping.

Angie tried diligently to think of something more to say. "I went food shopping on my way home.''

"Hey, let me help you in with the bags.''

Her knees got weak at the thought of him coming inside the empty apartment with her. "No, really. I can handle it.'' She was becoming as squishy as a jellyfish.

Sonny smiled thinly. "I'm still your brother-in-law.'' Inside his head, a voice was talking to him the whole time he was talking to her. *Can't you take no for an answer?*

When she made no move, he took a hand from his pocket and placed it lightly on her elbow. Giving her an assist, he led her back to her car. Angie fumbled for a moment until she got the key to work in the lock of her trunk.

Sonny tested the weight of each paper bag before he grabbed the three that were heaviest. Angie took out the last two. She waited while he went to his car to get Lindsay's teddy bear.

They walked the path lined with short, frozen evergreens, and went into the building. The process of taking the groceries in would have taken her, at the very least, three trips.

Angie put one bag down, freeing a hand to unlock the door. She picked the bag back up. Sonny closed the door behind him with a bump of his shoulder. He followed her to the kitchen.

Angie put her bags on the table. Sonny did the same. Angie took her pea jacket off, and dropped it to one of the cane-backed kitchen chairs.

Sonny took her in at a quick glance. She had on an oversize sweater. Her jeans were tucked into her boots.

"I understand that you and Richie have been getting real close," he commented as she started to unpack.

"I guess sort of close." Her eyes came to his. She held a head of lettuce midair. "How do you know?"

"I had drinks with Frankie." Wanting to break eye contact, Sonny began unpacking another one of the bags. "He said everyone in the family likes him."

"Well . . ." Angie fixed her gaze on a box of cereal. "I guess no matter how old you are, you still want your family to approve."

In the silence that ensued, they both unloaded the bags.

"He's very interesting," Angie said finally.

"Good." Sonny nodded and shrugged.

Angie opened the freezer over her refrigerator. Without considering the idea that he was stalling, Sonny began to hand her perishables. Working together, they put all the food items away. Angie folded the brown paper bags and stored them in the cabinet under the sink.

Sonny trained his eyes on the cleared tabletop. "I guess I'll be going." He'd never taken his coat off, though he had unbuttoned it.

"How about a cup of coffee first?" She wasn't trying to detain him, she told herself. She was being polite. It was cold out.

Sonny took a split second to make a judgment call. "Okay, if it isn't any trouble."

"It isn't any trouble." Angie moved quickly to set up a fresh pot of coffee. "Why don't you take your coat off?"

Sonny dropped his camel-hair coat over her jacket. He pulled out a chair and sat down. Angie took two mugs from one of the cabinets and set them on the counter. Keeping her back to the kitchen table, she watched the warm brown liquid drip into the glass decanter. It came through quickly. She'd only filled it for four cups.

Sonny spent those few minutes gearing himself up. He rubbed a hand across his face and through his hair. He wanted her to be happy, and she'd given him every indication that she was. He'd had plenty of time to mull over their situation. He'd even traded places with her in his mind. Given his career, she had every reason to stay fixated on the heartbreak he might have caused her in the end. Mentally, he tried to bow out gracefully.

Angie came to the table with the mugs filled. She'd fixed hers with milk and sugar. She knew he drank his black.

"Thanks," he said after she'd sat down across from him.

"Gee . . ." Angie sighed. "I'm uncomfortable. Are you?"

"Very." One of the facets he liked best about her was her point-blank manner.

Angie nodded. "I'm even more than that."

"I'm extreme to the max," he teased her lightly.

Angie tossed him a comical expression. "You can't win this one. I'm more than that, but I don't know what to call it. Is there such a thing as extremer to the max?"

Sonny grinned. "We could try talking it out. It might help."

"Yeah." She realized that she hadn't even taken a sip of her coffee. She put her fingers to the handle of the mug, but she didn't lift it. Instead, she gave him a cautionary look. "Frankie told me that you've been dating quite a bit."

Sonny glanced down. "Frankie gave me the impression that he was getting annoyed with us communicating through him."

Angie was fully aware that Sonny hadn't come forth with an answer. "Are you going out tonight?"

"Yes." His eyes drifted back to her. "Are you?"

"Yes." Angie was struck by another surge of discomfort.

"With Richie?" Sonny wasn't thrilled about the way he was handling himself. How many times did he have to push this around?

Angie nodded. Her neck felt stiff. "Sonny, you are being careful, aren't you?" Her voice became low and intense.

Her question paralyzed him for a minute and a half. "You mean . . ." he stammered.

Quite quickly, Angie realized he'd misinterpreted. She turned scarlet. "I didn't mean that . . . I meant at work."

"Sure." He tipped back his chair, raising the front legs from the floor. He wanted to put his palms to her cheeks to cool her flush, but his hands were sweaty.

Angie raised an arm to her face and ducked her head. "Well . . . I'm embarrassed."

Sonny did his best to help her out. It wasn't easy, with his mind hooked on the possibility of her needing to heed her own advice. "It was a good question either way."

"True." Angie dropped her arm to reveal that her face was still colored a high pink.

"I have an idea." Sonny took a breath to speculate the wisdom of what he was about to suggest.

"What?" Angie prodded when he paused.

"Why don't we double-date tonight?" Warning bells were clanging the *1812 Overture* in his head. He ignored them. Seeing her with Richie . . . seeing how they interacted was important to him.

There was silence. Angie pondered his proposal. Could she stand seeing him with someone else?

It was a stupid idea, Sonny decided while he waited. "Don't sweat it. Forget I asked... It's just that I'd hate us to lose the friendship we've established."

His last remark convinced her. "Let's do it. Richie made a dinner reservation at LaSalle. They have a band there on Saturday nights. It's in White Plains. Do you know the place?"

"I know it." Sonny smiled faintly. Why was he doing this to himself? "What time is the reservation?"

"Eight o'clock." Was he dating one woman or a variety of women? Frankie hadn't been any help when she'd questioned him on that point.

"We'll meet there." Sonny got to his feet and put on his coat. "I'll call and tell them there will be four of us." He had another thought. "Do you want to see how Richie feels about this first?"

Angie shook her head. "I'm sure he won't object." She had more than enough to do to deal with herself. "What about your date?"

"She won't mind."

They endured an awkward moment, then Sonny saluted a goodbye and headed out of the kitchen.

Angie took a half hour longer to dress than she'd originally allotted herself. She kept Richie waiting, but he'd come fifteen minutes early. He hadn't been overjoyed when she'd mentioned they were going to be double dating. She'd observed dismay on his face before he'd covered up.

"I haven't seen you in that dress before," Richie said.

"It's new." She'd seen herself in six new outfits within the last hour and a half. She'd gone shopping with Nancy two weeks ago. Why had everything looked so much better on her in the store dressing room with Nancy? Tonight, nothing had looked right. The cream-colored wool dress that she'd decided on, with no more time to spare, did draw notice to her curvy assets—as well as her liabilities. Short of stuffing her bra, there wasn't any dress that was going to do anything for her on top. Just how far had Lisa had her hand out from her chest when she was describing that woman she'd seen Sonny with before Thanksgiving?

"Are we ready to go?" Richie glanced impatiently at his watch.

Sonny was already there when Angie and Richie arrived. He was sitting at the bar just inside the entry. Angie and Sonny spotted each other at the same time. Richie checked his coat and Angie's coat, and they walked into the lounge. Fluorescent lighting was recessed into the ceiling throwing down dimmed illumination. The air was permeated with the smell of cigarette smoke and Continental cuisine. There was laughter here and there, and low conversation. The atmosphere was cozy.

"Sonny," Richie acknowledged, putting his hand out.

Sonny got to his feet. "Richie," Sonny replied, cataloging the insurance agent's merits. His dark hair was clipped professionally close. He had a strong chin in a face that radiated confidence. However, he wasn't as tall as Sonny remembered from the one other brief time they'd met. Sardonically, Sonny wondered how long it would take for Richie to work a sales pitch into the conversation.

Angie was taking a survey of Sonny's companion. She had turned on her stool to face the group. She couldn't have been more than twenty-four. She had clear skin, bright hazel eyes and a pouty mouth that was outlined in a very deep red and filled in with a shade a tint lighter. Her straight hair, a dark brown, was cut short and combed easy. The style didn't require any attention. She was pretty, and had a good figure—not as good as Lisa had described, though. Of course, this might not be the same woman Lisa had seen him with.

"Faith," Sonny said. "I'd like you to meet Angie and Richie."

Faith got to her feet, and pleasantries were exchanged along with handclasps. Angie tried her hardest to think sarcastically, but nothing came to mind. Faith had, what seemed to be, a genuine smile, and the teal blue dress that showed off her figure was trim, tailored and subdued. She wasn't a "bimbette," Angie conceded grudgingly.

"Our table will be ready in about twenty minutes," Sonny said.

"Angie, can I order you a glass of wine?" Richie asked.

"All right."

Sonny watched the smile she gave Richie along with her reply. Then he beckoned her to the stool he'd vacated as Faith sat back down. "Sit down."

"Thank you." Angie circumspectly smiled his way as she accepted. However, instead of looking at his face, she kept her eyes on the knot of his tie at the collar of his white shirt. She had to have been crazy to agree to this evening. Her body was a bundle of rawly strung nerves.

Richie moved into the rail to catch the bartender's eye.

Sonny picked up the scotch and soda he'd been drinking.

Off to the side, four musicians in dinner jackets stepped up to a platform. Their first selection was a bluesy number, and the lead singer had a pleasant smoky voice.

The bartender got to their end and Richie ordered two glasses of Chablis. "I understand from Frankie that you're a hockey fan," Richie said, engaging Sonny's attention. "I'm a diehard Islander fan myself."

The two women eyed each other.

"Sonny is always taking about his two nieces," Faith commented conversationally.

Angie smiled. Behind her, she could hear Sonny and Richie bonding over sports. She liked hockey herself, and did try to keep half an ear on the conversation.

"...not a trade I would have made," Sonny was saying.

"My sentiments exactly," Richie answered.

Sonny and Richie stepped away from the bar to make room for a couple of new arrivals to place an order.

Angie turned more fully to Faith. "Have you known Sonny long?"

"About two years. We work together. I'm still an officer. I am hoping to make detective." Faith sipped her Bloody Mary.

Angie was startled. "I would never have guessed that you were with the police department."

Faith laughed. "I'd worry if I looked like a cop when I was dressing civilian."

Angie smiled. Faith was natural and up-front. Angie understood what Sonny must see in her. Only, why had it taken him two years to see it?

Faith drew on the straw in her glass. "I had a good picture of you in my mind. Sonny talks as much about you as he does about your daughters."

Angie was denied a follow-up to that statement. Just as she was about to speak, Richie and Sonny moved in again.

"Our table is ready," Sonny said.

Angie and Faith slid from their stools. Drinks in hand, they all walked through an arch trellised with fake greenery, to be seated.

Their meals took awhile. They talked about movies and TV shows. Angie remembered Sonny giving her a lesson on small talk. She thought about the singles party they'd gone to, recalling the way they'd wound up in each other's arms that night....

"I know Sonny's favorite movie is *Lethal Weapon*,"

Faith said, smiling as she added, "I'd have to say it's mine, too."

Angie wanted to say, "give me a break," but bit her tongue. Though she hadn't wanted to, she'd already warmed to Faith. She couldn't fault her for wanting to score a point with Sonny.

"The best movie ever made," Richie said, "is *Casablanca*."

Sonny's scalp prickled. He eyed Angie, but she only connected with him fleetingly. So Richie played the game... So what? Men played games. Women played games. What else was new?

"Angie." Faith looked her way. "What's your favorite movie?"

"I guess I like the movies of the 1940s best." Angie's head ached, and she would have preferred to sit quietly.

Faith prodded, "You have to pick something more recent."

Angie fidgeted with her napkin. "*When Harry Met Sally*. I haven't seen anything since then that made me feel as good."

Faith puckered her bottom lip. "I hope it doesn't take my Mr. Right that long to figure out we're made for each other."

Angie labeled the glance Faith gave Sonny as decidedly provocative. She didn't let herself check out Sonny's expression.

The food arrived and they all concentrated on eating. In the lounge, the band kept blasting up-tempo tunes.

"Let's dance," Faith said to Sonny over the cappuccino they'd each ordered after dinner.

"Shall we?" Richie suggested to Angie.

As couples, they made their way to the dance floor, and joined a line dance already in progress. They were winded by the time the set ended and the music slowed.

"I don't want to go back to the table, yet," Faith said, tugging on Sonny's arm.

Smiling at Angie, Richie was still raring to go. "Come on. One more song," Richie said, pulling her closer.

Faith assumed the position and Sonny fit her into his arms. Angie allowed Richie to direct her into place. The dance floor got crowded, and neither couple was able to do much more than sway side by side. One tune blended into another, and Angie let her thoughts drift. She was mentally worn-out.

A song or so later, Faith said playfully, "May I cut in?"

The trade of dance partners took place before Angie could counter the idea. She was immediately stiff and tense in Sonny's arms.

For his part, Sonny tried not to hold her too close. They got bumped together so often in the crowd, though, that he gave up the fight. Their hips melded closer with each small step. Angie tried to keep Faith and Richie in her sight, just to have something else to concentrate on. But there were too many bodies in the way.

Angie listed to the right as Sonny led to the left. She cleared her throat. "Something wrong? You're so quiet."

"You're quiet, too," Sonny answered. As far as he was concerned, conversation wasn't necessary. Their bodies were already talking.

It took Angie awhile to decide what to say. "Faith is very nice."

Sonny nodded. "Richie is nice, too."

"Are you having a good time?"

Sonny considered responding truthfully, but he didn't. "Sure," he lied. "Are you having a good time?"

"Absolutely," Angie fabricated.

"We'll have to do this again." He wasn't sure how he got the words out.

Angie cleared of her throat again. "Definitely."

They judiciously maneuvered not to look each other in the face, but he impulsively pulled her closer. For Angie, the feel of him was becoming painfully wonderful and familiar.

Just when they each thought they weren't going to survive the closeness of their bodies any longer, the song ended.

"It seems to have gotten very warm in here," Sonny said as they split.

"Yes," Angie agreed, her pulse running amok.

Sonny loosened the knot of his tie and undid the top button on his shirt. "I guess we should go back to the table . . ."

Sonny put a steering hand at the small of Angie's back. He used his other hand to clear the way.

Faith and Richie were already at the table. Angie and Sonny sat down. Richie strung his arm over the back of Angie's chair. Sonny wondered whether

Richie was being casual or making a statement. He knew he had no business wondering. More than that, he had no business reacting.

Sonny looked over at Faith. He did like her. Their relationship had always been satisfying. Work gave them a strong tie. There had never been anything more than friendship between them. He'd never felt any sparks. She had an on-again, off-again relationship with a cop out of a precinct downtown.

Faith looked directly at Sonny, and they smiled at each other.

Catching the interplay, Angie's heart bounced around in her chest.

"Has everyone finished their Christmas shopping?" Richie asked. "What have we got now, ten more days?"

"I still have a way to go," Faith answered.

"I haven't found the time to get started," Sonny said.

"I've made a small dent," Angie put in.

Richie stayed focused on Angie. "Do you put up a real tree?"

"Yes." Angie brightened. Christmas with the girls was the one thing she was looking forward to.

"Let me help you pick one out," Richie said.

"All right." Angie smiled.

On top of the table, Sonny put his hand over Faith's hand.

"I think I'll put up a real tree for once," Faith said, lacing her fingers with Sonny's.

"I'll take you for one," Sonny said quickly, rolling out the charm.

They wore out the subject of Christmas trees and decorations in the next half hour. Finally, Richie mentioned the time. It was nearly one-thirty. The men divided the check, and after putting their coats on, they all said brief goodbyes. As couples, they parted in the street to hurry to their cars. The night was bitingly cold.

Angie slouched in the passenger seat of Richie's car. She tipped her head back. Richie slipped in a cassette tape, and Eric Clapton undercut the quiet with "Knocking on Heaven's Door."

"I liked your brother-in-law and his girlfriend," Richie remarked. "But I do like it better when we go out by ourselves."

"Me too." Angie sighed, knowing she didn't mean it the way he'd meant it.

At that, Richie took his eyes from the road to send over a pleased smile. "You seem tired."

"Yes." Angie nodded. *Despondent* and *depleted* would have been better words.

"I don't mind if you want to close your eyes while I drive."

Angie did. She absolutely didn't feel like talking.

Richie parked his car near the path to Angie's building. He helped her out. She'd opened her eyes as soon as he'd turned the motor off. They walked to her door. Angie sluggishly raised her head, making herself accessible to a good-night kiss.

Richie bent and placed his mouth at her ear. "Let me come in," he murmured.

Instantly alert, Angie shook her head. "No."

"Why not?"

Angie gulped. "Because..."

Richie ran his thumb along the side of her face. "I promise to stop if you tell me to stop. I don't think I've made a secret of it. I've fallen for you."

"Richie—I'm sorry," Angie blurted out. "You're terrific and all that, but it just hasn't happened for me. I've *wanted* it to happen."

Richie pulled back. "Are you aware that you've been leading me on?"

"I guess I have been." She'd never come on to him deliberately, but she'd been aware that he was attracted to her, and she hadn't headed him off. "It could still happen for me." She felt she needed to say something nice.

"Do you really think there's any chance of that?" His tone was edged with annoyance. She could tell she'd hurt his feelings.

Angie considered her choices. There were only two answers to choose from. "No," she murmured.

"Then there doesn't seem to be anything else to say."

Angie watched Richie stride away while she rooted in her handbag for her key.

He pivoted toward her when he was halfway down the hall. "Listen, if you have anymore insurance business, do me a favor and take it elsewhere."

The extent of his anger shook her. Angie dropped her key. He was out of her sight by the time she picked it up.

Chapter Ten

Observing his fellow New Yorkers, Sonny stood at the corner of Church Street and Canal on the Lower East Side. The almost perpetual New York vehemence seemed to give way to a truce during the Christmas season. Even the cabs and trucks that ceaselessly bullied pedestrians toed the line now. Streets were, as usual, littered and crowded, but the glow of the holiday trim and store decorations worked a magical transformation. Everyone looked happier and more attractive, charged with excitement and goodwill.

It was nearly four o'clock. Sonny was on loan to a precinct in the city. He'd come straight from work in a suit, shirt, tie and topcoat.

There were only four more shopping days left until Christmas. He'd made most of his purchases. All he had left on his list was a last big gift for Melissa and

Lindsay. For that, he wanted Angie's approval. He'd already bought the girls a bunch of small items.

A cab pulled up. The rear door opened a second later. Angie alighted and headed his way. The sight of her charged him with excitement any day of the year.

Sonny knew he shouldn't, but he allowed himself to fantasize that there wasn't a stalemate and an insurance agent between them. It was his Christmas present to himself.

She stood before him in jeans tucked into her boots, the collar of her pea jacket pulled up under her hair and a powder-blue wool scarf around her neck. Her eyes looked bright, her cheeks rosy from the cold. She looked a little breathless and very kissable.

Sonny spoke first. "How are you?"

"Good." Angie held up a hand to keep her hair from blowing in her face. "How are you?"

"Good. I tried to call you a number of times, but I kept getting your machine." He hadn't seen her since the night they'd double-dated.

Angie's expression became distressed. "The only message I got from you was the one you left yesterday asking me if I could meet you here. I'll have to get my machine checked."

"I didn't leave any other messages. I guessed you were busy. Frankie told me that you and the girls were fine, so I figured I didn't have to ask."

Angie caught at her scarf as it flapped between them. She was glad that she hadn't told anyone in the family that she wasn't seeing Richie Walker anymore. "Have you been busy?"

"Very." Sonny nodded.

There was a verbal gap in the conversation, but their eyes continued to speak. "Well...hi," Angie managed to say.

Sonny had to haul out every ounce of his restraint to keep his hands off of her. "Hi," he responded. "Who's watching the girls?"

"I drove in to Teddy and Quinn's with them. They're just in Soho. I figured it was easier to leave my car there and take a cab rather than have to look for parking."

"I'll drive you back."

"Okay." Angie's mouth lifted at the corners.

The frigid cold assaulted and invaded their bodies. They stood gazing at each other, unaware of the glacial chill.

Sonny savored her face. "After shopping, we could go for dinner, if you like?"

Angie knew she was punishing herself as she said, "That would be nice." She supposed she should ask after Faith, but she didn't.

"The place is just up the street." He was anxious to get going now...now that he had something more to look forward to.

Angie walked at his side. "Who told you about this place?"

"Some of the guys I work with. They said the only way to go is wholesale if you're looking for something big. They open for the police and fire department the last week before Christmas. You have to call and make an appointment with them, which I did." He took her hand and tucked it through his arm. "There's some ice patches around," he said, giving her an excuse for his grip. He thought he should probably ask her how Richie was, but he didn't want to bring up his name.

Being this close to Sonny made Angie breathe rapidly. "I'm not going to let you go haywire with this gift." She'd been trying very hard to tell herself that she was happy he'd finally found someone. So far, she hadn't succeeded.

Sonny gave Angie a half smile. "It's been a while since you and I sparred. I don't know about you, but I've missed it."

Angie's heart did a jig. "Don't tease."

"I'm not teasing." Sonny's smile reached his blue eyes.

"I'm stubborn and a pain in the neck. We both know that..." She trailed off. What had he ever seen in her?

"True." He grinned crookedly at her. "But in a good way." He knew he was taking selecting a present for the girls a little far, but damned if he wasn't going to enjoy it. Did Richie enjoy being around her as much as he did?

"Where's a tape recorder when you need one?" She joked back, all tingly inside.

"This is it." Sonny stopped walking, bringing Angie to a halt at the entrance to the Edwards Toy Factory.

Sonny dropped her arm to open the door. Angie hated when he let go of her.

She preceded him inside. If he could have come up with an excuse to hold on to her again, he would have. It wasn't for lack of trying that nothing came to mind.

"Are we supposed to just browse around?" Angie whispered.

There were cubicles just inside with desks beyond them, but there wasn't anyone around that they could see.

"I don't see why not, unless someone stops us. Let's hit the showroom and see what happens." Sonny was reading the lettering on the glass doors straight ahead.

Again, Sonny held open a door for Angie. The room was large. There was a conference table, but no chairs. The walls were layered with shelves filled with toys. In the factory behind the showroom, a light went off, signaling their presence.

"They both have enough dolls." Angie was still speaking in a hushed tone. "I've already bought them each the one they've been seeing every five minutes on TV. You know what would be nice . . . doll carriages. I wonder if they have doll carriages here?"

Sonny smiled. "I got doll carriages for them."

Angie tilted her head to give him a scolding look, playacting that she wasn't on edge around him. "Then what are we doing here? You got them a big gift. That's enough."

Sonny shook his head. "I want them to have something else . . . something more than dolls and carriages . . . something that will really knock them out. A kid is supposed to be knocked out at Christmas."

Angie groaned, then smiled. "Are you forgetting how old they are? They get knocked out very easily. Are you looking for something that *you* can play with? Is that it?"

I'd like to play with you, he said with his eyes.

Angie felt the scintillating sexuality between them, and didn't know what to do. His teasing flirtatiousness was very hard on her.

Two men walked in on them. Both were bald and heavyset and looked to be anywhere between thirty and forty. They wore jeans and sweatshirts and the resemblance between them continued to their features.

Sonny showed his badge, and the brothers, Joe and Michael Edwards, introduced themselves. Sonny and Angie realized, as the exchange was made, that the men assumed they were husband and wife. Neither Angie nor Sonny corrected the assumption. For Sonny, the fantasy continued. For Angie, a fantasy began.

"Boys, girls?" Joe asked.

"Two girls," Sonny answered.

"Their ages?" Brother Michael used the same clipped manner of speech as brother Joe.

Angie responded this time. "One is almost five, and the other is almost two."

"Dolls, carriages . . ." Joe suggested.

"We've got the dolls and carriages," Sonny responded. "We're looking for something extra . . . something different."

"They're young." Michael put his thinking cap on.

"They're very bright." Sonny boasted as every father does while the mother glowed her agreement.

"Something educational?" Joe said, looking at Michael.

"That's a possibility," Sonny interjected. "But it has to be fun."

Joe tossed Michael a glance. "Are you thinking what I'm thinking?"

"Karaoke?" Michael asked. Joe nodded his head. "It's hot. The department stores have reordered three times."

"Six to eight," Michael reminded his brother of the labeling.

"They'll look, we'll see," was Joe's reply.

The brothers walked out the back door leaving Angie and Sonny looking at each other.

"Karaoke?" Angie flicked her eyebrow, feeling a little less uptight.

Sonny smiled. "We'll look, we'll see."

Angie giggled at Sonny's imitation.

Sonny laughed. Angie slapped her hand to his mouth, afraid the brothers might hear and guess the reason for their amusement. Only, Angie was having as much trouble cutting off her own giggles as she was Sonny's laughter.

"Will you stop it?" Angie sputtered.

Sonny's eyes still dancing, he lightly nipped her palm with his teeth. Impertinently, Angie pinched his nose before she took her hand away.

Sonny was just about to lasso her for a playful kiss when the brothers returned. It was just as well, Sonny told himself. He knew he didn't have the right to make that kind of move on her.

"We thought," Joe began, putting a small-scaled Karaoke on the table.

"A playhouse for the younger one," Michael finished his brother's sentence.

"One she can walk into," Joe elaborated.

"Comes unassembled," Michael warned.

"Love it." Sonny grinned at Angie.

"Price?" Angie asked, trying to keep from giggling again.

"Retail," Joe said. "Eighty-five . . . ninety-five."

Angie shook her head strenuously at Sonny.

"Wholesale?" Sonny inquired.

"Thirty-five," Michael decided after a silent eyeball discussion with Joe.

"We'll take one," Sonny said quickly, giving Angie a little-boy look.

Angie didn't know why she bothered to fuss, he melted her so easily. "How much is the Karaoke?"

"Look it over," Joe said.

"We'll talk," Michael added.

The brothers withdrew once more from the room.

Angie narrowed her gaze at Sonny. "The playhouse is enough for both of them."

Sonny had already lifted what looked like a thirteen-inch TV off the table. It was light enough for a child to handle. "Let's look," he grinned at her, putting it back down. "We'll talk."

Teasingly, Angie screwed up her face.

"You're going to have to do better than that," Sonny winked and slipped a disc into the slot on top of the screen. He pressed down a lever marked A. "Itsy-Bitsy Spider" came out from the speaker at the bottom of the monitor while the words flashed across the screen. Sonny picked up the microphone attached by a cord. "Try it with me." Sonny gave Angie an exaggerated dose of coaxing with his eyes.

Angie stepped into his space, and smiled at him. Sonny put his arm around her to share the mike. They sang "Itsy-Bitsy Spider" together. Sonny stopped midway while Angie was holding on to a note.

"What?" Angie asked.

Sonny smiled. He'd quit singing to enjoy her vigorous rendition.

"You don't like my singing, is that it?"

He flashed his teeth. "I love your singing."

She hiked away from him, but she wasn't really upset. "Don't humor me. When I was in high school and we all had to sing in the chorus, Mr. Harris told me to just mouth the words. I don't understand, because I always sound okay to me."

"Come back here," Sonny said throatily.

Angie moseyed back, intentionally taking her time.

Sonny tapped the tip of her nose and ran his finger slowly across her mouth. The sensation of his touch at her lips gave Angie goose bumps. She had to do something to distract herself from his attack. She pressed lever B at the top of the monitor.

This time the lyrics came out of the speaker along with the music.

"Wow!" Sonny exclaimed. "Melissa can get a head start on reading. She'll learn the words as she hears them, and then she'll be able to recognize them on the screen when she just plays the music. Don't fight me on this, this is terrific..."

Before Angie got a word out, Sonny hugged her impulsively.

"We could chip in together." Angie didn't know where she found the strength and sense to pull away. She'd had to draw very deep inside herself to do it.

"Sorry," Sonny mumbled, stepping away, undercutting his elation.

Angie nodded, wishing she hadn't made him feel that he had to apologize.

There was a pause between them that grew uncomfortable.

Lacking words, Sonny tried another disc in the slot.

"The Farmer In The Dell" was playing as the brothers came back into the room. Joe was carrying a large flat cardboard box twirled with twine. Michael brought in a square box with a picture of the Karaoke on the front side.

Sonny took his checkbook out of his inside coat pocket.

"Thought you'd want both," Michael said, handing Sonny an invoice.

Angie looked over Sonny's shoulder as he wrote out a check for an amount that was double the cost of the playhouse. She decided she'd write out a check for half the charge once they sat down to eat. She wanted to hold on to the fantasy that they were married...at least a little longer.

"I can carry the Karaoke," Angie was saying when the front door of the showroom opened, and, of all people, Faith walked in. She was accompanied by two men who stepped in behind her.

"Angie, how are you?" Faith smiled brightly.

"Good." Angie's breath was caught in her throat. "And you?"

"Great," Faith answered.

"Didn't know you were coming today," one of the men said, addressing Sonny.

"We could have all come together," the other man added.

Sonny held a grimace in check. He was annoyed to have the three raining on his parade.

He introduced Angie to two of his co-workers, Dave and Jimmy. Then he tried for a quick exit. "Have fun. We're going for dinner. We're both starving."

Jimmy staved him off. "Hang around. We're going for dinner in Little Italy after we finish here. We can all go together. We're each only looking for one toy. It won't take us long."

Sonny thought of saying that he didn't eat Italian food out, but Faith would have nailed him on that lie. Short of being rude, Sonny couldn't think of a way to get himself uncornered.

Angie made up her mind that there wasn't any way that she could be around Sonny and Faith. Once had been more than enough for her. She turned to Sonny.

"I really should get back to the girls," she told him. "You hang out. I'll get a cab."

Sonny saw the stubborn jut of Angie's chin. "I'll go out with you, and get you a cab." He knew there wasn't any way he was going to change her mind.

Sonny found a cab too quickly. Angie said, "See you," as he opened the back passenger door for her.

"Is it all right if I bring the gifts for the girls over Christmas Eve after they've gone to sleep?" he asked as she settled herself inside.

"Sure," Angie answered, then leaned forward to give the cabbie Quinn and Teddy's address.

Sonny closed the door and watched the cab pull away. He stood on the sidewalk awhile longer, even after he couldn't see it anymore.

Using his elbow, Sonny rapped on Angie's apartment door. It was nine p.m. on Christmas Eve. He had his hands full.

Angie opened the door after a quick glance through the peephole. She was expecting him. He'd called first to be sure the girls were in bed.

"I have a few more things to get from my car," he said, smiling softly at her. Threads of tinsel that she'd used to decorate her Christmas tree were caught in her hair. There was tinsel on her plaid flannel shirt and corduroy jeans. Her cheeks were flushed. He guessed she'd been rushing to finish up.

Angie took a wrapped carton from him that she could tell contained the Karaoke. Sonny leaned the still-uncrated playhouse against one of the foyer walls.

They got caught up looking at each other, both with their hearts reacting, both momentarily mute. An empty feeling crept into each of them unexpectedly. The holiday high and the thought of the girls' excitement on Christmas morning wasn't enough to fill them.

"Is that Santa Claus?" Melissa yelled from her bedroom.

"No," Angie called back. She smiled, making a stab at recovering her enthusiasm. "It's Uncle Sonny. I thought you were asleep."

"Uncle Sonny, can I come give you a good-night kiss?" Melissa asked, transparently. Sonny couldn't help grinning.

Angie shook her head at him, pointing to the tree where she'd just finished laying out her gifts for the girls.

Sonny winked back at her, and they both felt saved from the emptiness for at least a time. "I'll come to you for that kiss, Moonbeam, just as soon as I warm up." Then he whispered, "I'll be right back."

Angie left the front door open. She brought the Karaoke to the tree, and then dragged in the playhouse. Sonny returned with two more unwrapped cartons, each with a picture of a doll carriage. "One more trip," he said in a low voice, and was gone again. When next he arrived, he was toting two shopping bags. He closed the door behind him and came into the living room. Angie had already brought the doll carriages in from the foyer, one at a time.

Sonny unzipped his navy parka and took it off. He massaged his hands to warm them up. He did the same to his face. "I'm going to get that kiss from Melissa. No peeking into my shopping bags." Bantering helped him keep his gaze off her mouth.

Angie lifted her eyes heavenward. "I'm not going to peek."

"Yeah, right." He grinned. "On second thought, you're coming with me." He took her hand and made her come along. Angie pretended to put up a struggle, wanting to be playful.

Sonny sat down on the side of Melissa's bed. The sleeves of his denim shirt were rolled up and his jeans had the comfortable fit that came after many washings.

Angie stood next to him. Lindsay was fast asleep in her crib. Sonny bent down, and Melissa gave him a wet kiss on his cheek and a tight hug. He reciprocated with equal vim and tenderness.

"Did Mommy tell you the story of the night before Christmas?" he asked, keeping his voice low.

Melissa nodded. "But I forget it. Can you tell me again?"

Angie and Sonny gave each other amused looks. "All right," Sonny conceded.

"Can you tell me in the living room?" Melissa asked. "Cause you could wake up Lindsay."

Sonny smiled at Angie. "I don't think Melissa needs grade school. We can send her right to college."

"Definitely." Angie grinned, relaxing.

Was she going to see Richie later that night? Sonny wondered. His gut clenched at the thought.

He looked back at Melissa. "I'll whisper it close to your ear. You have to close your eyes and promise to go right to sleep after I finish."

"I promise, Uncle Sonny."

Sonny laid his head down next to Melissa's. "'Twas the night before Christmas and all through the house..."

Angie tiptoed from the room. The sight and sound of Sonny with Melissa tore her apart. The waterworks came as she rushed to her bathroom.

"She's asleep," Sonny said a little later, finding Angie sitting in front of the tree with her knees bent to her face. She looked stricken and sad, and he wished he knew why, so he could fix whatever needed fixing. He sat down next to her and listened quietly to her shallow, fluttering breaths.

He picked a strand of tinsel out of her hair. "If it's all right with you, I'd like to put the carriages and the playhouse together before I leave."

Angie nodded. She didn't trust herself to speak without crying. She was certain that it was his intention to spend part of Christmas Eve with Faith.

Sonny didn't move, though he was instucting himself to get started. "I suppose you're expecting company?"

Angie shook her head.

Sonny did some fancy juggling with his head and his heart before he got his next question out. "Richie isn't coming over?"

"No." Angie tightened her hands around her knees.

Sonny agonized before he asked, "Will he be here in the morning?"

Angie's eyes flickered. She inhaled deeply. "I'm not seeing him anymore." She didn't have any energy left to play make-believe. "But I don't want you to make me your problem again."

"Oh, Angie," Sonny groaned. "You've never been a problem to me. I love you. Haven't you got it yet?"

Angie dropped her face to his shoulder, looking to hide the moisture overwhelming her eyes. "But Faith . . ."

"We're just friends. We've never been *more* than just friends. Do you think she would have instigated that you and I dance together the night we doubledated if she and I were more than just friends? She was trying to help me out."

He did his best to embrace her carefully. He wasn't going to risk losing her closeness with too intimate a touch.

Slowly, Angie absorbed that information. "It isn't just that you're a cop. I don't know how to make it feel right loving you and still loving Rick . . ."

"Angie . . ." Sonny said her name raggedly. "I don't expect you to ever stop loving Rick. I love Rick, too. But, Angie, every relationship is unique, and what you and I have is special and just between us. You didn't love Melissa any less when Lindsay was born. I think it's sort of the same thing."

His answer and understanding infused her heart with longing. She marveled at how wise he was. "What do we do now?"

He was willing to turn himself inside out for her. "I could find other work..."

Angie's head shot up. "No, Sonny... I'd never ask that of you. I know how much it means to you to be on the force."

He clutched her shoulders. "Do you love me, Angie?" He had to hear it again.

"Yes, Sonny." She felt a renewed sense of even stronger longing. "I love you so much, it hurts."

Sonny's Adam's apple rode up and down. "Angie, I want to be married to you. I want to bring up the girls with you. I want a child with you. I want us to be a family. We could have so much."

Angie closed her eyes tightly while she battled herself hopelessly. "I can't get past it, Sonny. I just can't..."

She felt bereft when he took his hands from her. She knew when he got to his feet. She heard the rasp as he zipped his jacket. She trembled uncontrollably, listening to his footsteps on the foyer floor.

He didn't look back at her as he opened the door. He closed it softly.

Wait, Sonny, she wanted to scream. And then she must have, because she heard herself. Her eyes flew open as she quickly jumped up.

"I'm still here." He was standing in the foyer, leaning back against the door, his hands jammed into the pockets of his parka. "You're not the only one who's stubborn. I can't fall in love and push it out of my mind. The way I see it, we're just going to have to keep at it until we work this out."

She walked to him with tears streaming down her face.

He wiped at her eyes. "I know you're scared," he said gently. "But I'm not going to let you give up on us. What we have together is special and rare. It's a gift and it's not right to just throw it all away."

In her heart, Angie knew what he was saying was true. Yet, she couldn't find the words to answer him.

"I can't give you any guarantees, honey," Sonny added, "except that I'm always going to be crazy about you."

Sniffling, Angie threaded her fingers into his hair.

He pressed her firmly and securely between his spread legs, flattening her to his rigid body. "I'll call you every hour on the hour when I'm at work."

"You will?" She kissed the side of his face, seeking and fevered.

"I promise . . ."

"You may not always be able to." She pushed one hand between them to get to the zipper of his parka. She needed to be closer to the warmth of his body.

"But I'll always try . . ." He gave her just enough space to accomplish her goal. When she'd succeeded, she pulled his jacket apart and wrapped her arms around his neck tenaciously.

"Promise me that." Her eyes burned into his.

"I promise . . ."

She kissed him. They pressed their bodies together, each fighting to be the one to give the most.

Groaning, Sonny yanked her fiercely away from his hips. "You are going to marry me, aren't you?"

"Yes, Sonny." She touched his face.

"When?" he demanded.

"Quickly," Angie answered.

"Good." He gave her the grin she knew so well. Then he drew her back where she needed to be, in the circle of his arms.

*   *   *   *   *

HE'S MORE THAN A MAN, HE'S ONE OF OUR

REBEL DAD
Kristin Morgan

When Linc Rider discovered he was a father, he was determined to find his son and take him back. But he found that Eric already had a home with his adoptive mother, Jillian Fontenot. The choice wouldn't be easy: take the boy from such a beautiful, loving woman or leave his son behind. And soon it was too late to tell Jillian the real reason he'd spent so many days in her home—and in her arms....

Join Linc in his search for family—and love—in Kristin Morgan's REBEL DAD. Available in January—only from Silhouette Romance!

Fall in love with our **Fabulous Fathers!**

Silhouette
ROMANCE™

FF194

Take 4 bestselling love stories FREE

Plus get a FREE surprise gift!

UNDER THE MISTLETOE

Where's the best place to find love this holiday season? UNDER THE MISTLETOE, *of course! In this special collection, some of your favorite authors celebrate the joy of the season and the thrill of romance.*

#976 DADDY'S ANGEL by Annette Broadrick
#977 ANNIE AND THE WISE MEN by Lindsay Longford
#978 THE LITTLEST MATCHMAKER by Carla Cassidy
#979 CHRISTMAS WISHES by Moyra Tarling
#980 A PRECIOUS GIFT by Jayne Addison
#981 ROMANTICS ANONYMOUS by Lauryn Chandler

Available in December from

Silhouette
R O M A N C E™

Christmas Classics

Share in the joys of finding happiness and exchanging the ultimate gift—love—in full-length classic holiday treasures by two bestselling authors

JOAN HOHL
EMILIE RICHARDS

Available in December at
your favorite retail outlet.

Only from  *where passion lives.*

SILHOUETTE.... Where Passion Lives

Don't miss these Silhouette favorites by some of our most popular authors!
And now, you can receive a discount by ordering two or more titles!

Silhouette Desire®

#05751	THE MAN WITH THE MIDNIGHT EYES BJ James	$2.89	☐
#05763	THE COWBOY Cait London	$2.89	☐
#05774	TENNESSEE WALTZ Jackie Merritt	$2.89	☐
#05779	THE RANCHER AND THE RUNAWAY BRIDE Joan Johnston	$2.89	☐

Silhouette Intimate Moments®

#07417	WOLF AND THE ANGEL Kathleen Creighton	$3.29	☐
#07480	DIAMOND WILLOW Kathleen Eagle	$3.39	☐
#07486	MEMORIES OF LAURA Marilyn Pappano	$3.39	☐
#07493	QUINN EISLEY'S WAR Patricia Gardner Evans	$3.39	☐

Silhouette Shadows®

#27003	STRANGER IN THE MIST Lee Karr	$3.50	☐
#27007	FLASHBACK Terri Herrington	$3.50	☐
#27009	BREAK THE NIGHT Anne Stuart	$3.50	☐
#27012	DARK ENCHANTMENT Jane Toombs	$3.50	☐

Silhouette Special Edition®

#09754	THERE AND NOW Linda Lael Miller	$3.39	☐
#09770	FATHER: UNKNOWN Andrea Edwards	$3.39	☐
#09791	THE CAT THAT LIVED ON PARK AVENUE Tracy Sinclair	$3.39	☐
#09811	HE'S THE RICH BOY Lisa Jackson	$3.39	☐

Silhouette Romance®

#08893	LETTERS FROM HOME Toni Collins	$2.69	☐
#08915	NEW YEAR'S BABY Stella Bagwell	$2.69	☐
#08927	THE PURSUIT OF HAPPINESS Anne Peters	$2.69	☐
#08952	INSTANT FATHER Lucy Gordon	$2.75	☐

	AMOUNT	$ _____
DEDUCT:	10% DISCOUNT FOR 2+ BOOKS	$ _____
	POSTAGE & HANDLING	$ _____
	($1.00 for one book, 50¢ for each additional)	
	APPLICABLE TAXES*	$ _____
	TOTAL PAYABLE	$ _____
	(check or money order—please do not send cash)	

To order, complete this form and send it, along with a check or money order for the total above, payable to Silhouette Books, to: *In the U.S.*: 3010 Walden Avenue, P.O. Box 9077, Buffalo, NY 14269-9077; *In Canada*: P.O. Box 636, Fort Erie, Ontario, L2A 5X3.

Name: _____

Address: _____ City: _____

State/Prov.: _____ Zip/Postal Code: _____

*New York residents remit applicable sales taxes.
Canadian residents remit applicable GST and provincial taxes.

SBACK-OD

Ⓥ Silhouette